Pirates
at
Mafeking Bay

The Tale of a Fisheries Inspector

BOB PIETSCH

 A catalogue record for this book is available from the National Library of Australia

Publisher:
ASPG (Australian Self Publishing Group)
P.O. Box 159, Calwell, ACT Australia 2905
Email: publishaspg@gmail.com
http://www.inspiringpublishers.com

National Library of Australia Cataloguing-in-Publication entry

Author: Pietsch, Bob

Title: **Pirates at Mafeking Bay/***Bob Pietsch*

ISBN: 978-1-922327-04-8 (print)
　　　978-1-922327-05-5 (eBook)

Genre: Rural Crime Fiction, Australian Crime Fiction

Dedication

T o Ian Rowell and Francis O'Connor.

On the 25th April 1985, Fisheries and Wildlife Officer Ian Rowell and Francis O'Connor lost their lives in a tragic boating accident off the Warrnambool coastline. In dedicating this book to Ian and Francis it is my hope readers learn something of the excitement and the dangers of being a fisheries inspector.

Francis's friend, Shannon McBride was also on the boat when it capsized. Shannon was working for the Victorian Archaeological Survey at the time and she later became the first female Fisheries and Wildlife Officer in Victoria.

The characters portrayed in this book are fictitious and probably not politically correct. (If they were politically correct they would not be fishermen). While the ideas for this book stem from my experiences as a Fisheries and Wildlife Officer up to about 1990, any resemblance to real persons, alive or dead, is purely coincidental.

Some real place names, circumstances and events have been used for context and setting but the majority of towns and places are also fictitious.

Chapter 1

The rough hand painted sign read "STEVENS IS A BASTARD." A blue Eureka Flag defiantly displayed the stars of the Southern Cross. It fluttered proudly on a pole in the front yard of a cement sheet and weather board house a couple of blocks from the beach. There were no trees, bushes or garden, just a lawn of buffalo grass that had grown up the chain link fencing and posts surrounding the front yard. The grass was more yellow than green, and in urgent need of water, fertilizer, a mower and a gardener.

'What's that all about?' Kirby Wellington asked his new boss.

'It should be Stephens with a "ph," Greg Bayliss explained. 'It's really the boss, Murray Stephens, from head office. Lincoln Campbell lives here. He's a professional fisherman and a real pirate. He has had a dirty on for years. It started when Murray booked him for selling undersized crayfish and the department prosecuted him. He's been prosecuted more than a few times since then too. I reckon if you're any good as an inspector here at Mafeking Bay you'll be next to write him up, maybe even within a few weeks. The sign's there to enlighten Lincoln's customers about the government, and of course, all us fisheries inspectors.

'Lincoln's got absolutely no idea about conservation. He thinks all fisheries laws were designed specifically so we can make his life miserable whenever we feel like it. He has two brothers, Michael and Bernard who are also professional fishermen. None of them would ever dream of looking after fish stocks today so they will be available tomorrow as well. The three of them just rape and pillage our natural environment and Lincoln, especially, thinks each and every fish in the sea in this part of the world are his. No one else matters and he doesn't give a rats if there are no fish left for our grandkids.

'Most of Lincoln's fish, big or little, are sold to customers who come here to his house. That's what the sign's about really, Lincoln's selfish, personal agenda.'

'Yeah, I've met a few people like that since I joined the job.' Kirby was thinking specifically about Maxwell Thomas Morrison, known to all and sundry as MT. Kirby and MT had had their share of encounters prior to Kirby being stationed at Mafeking Bay.

Kirby had been promoted from head office only a couple of weeks previously. Greg was now Kirby's officer-in-charge and the boss knew all about Lincoln Campbell, the fisherman who erected had the sign and flew the Eureka Flag. The two officers were on a tour of the district, with the senior man giving Kirby an insight into the rigours and joys of life at a country station.

As part of this mentor role, Greg argued to himself, it was legitimate for him to digress and tell his new charge "war stories" about his personal experiences and exploits in the job. For Kirby this was a pleasant interlude away from FRED, the office network computer terminal. FRED, that "Flippen Ridiculous Electronic Device," had been Kirby's constant companion since he began working with Greg. It was an understatement to say FRED had shown Kirby his new boss had one or two shortcomings. Unbeknown to Greg, it was often true his war stories helped develop an image in Kirby's mind. Greg was a public servant who had enjoyed the best of his career, had developed a well-earned reputation, a bad habit or two and was now slowing down as he approached the end of his working life.

In the months since Darren Wossfold left the job Kirby now occupied, Greg had been working by himself. In that time a mountain of log sheets, journals, reports, requisitions, accounts and summaries had piled up. Greg had deliberately left them for his new junior who he knew was appointed and just a few weeks away from starting work with him. His logic was this would be a good way for Kirby to learn what the real job was all about. Working at a country station was different from head office and Greg felt Kirby should learn that sooner rather than later.

Kirby consequently spent his first week at Mafeking Bay keying data into the computer and working himself into a bit of tizz in relation to being given all the crappy jobs. The need to finish his tertiary studies was constantly on his mind, and there was little time at home with his young family. They were all settling into a new house and all things associated with living in an unfamiliar town. Thankfully Kylie and Zac had settled into their new school and Nicky had some part time work at the local solicitor's office. There was simply no time for Kirby's cymbidium orchids or trips to footy or cricket matches.

Some of the older officers were vocal in their opposition to "bloody academics taking over," but even though Greg was not against his tertiary studies, Kirby knew saying anything about doing someone else's work and needing more personal time would be futile. Greg would simply point him to the "other duties as directed" statement in his position description.

Building a relationship with FRED in this way, however, did give Kirby a perspective into another facet of his new boss that perhaps Greg had not thought through. Or maybe he did. Maybe this was to see if Kirby picked up on it. It related to vehicle log-sheets. Kirby knew many of his colleagues did not make a single entry in their vehicle log book until the due date for submission. The data they used was then invented from diaries and fairyland.

As Kirby worked through Greg's log sheets he gained an impression the destinations were truthful but the documents contained a recurring apparent anomaly. The forms and the procedural manual both demanded the specific volumes of fuel purchases be recorded to an accuracy of two decimal places. Point nought one (0.01) of a litre is a very small volume, and Kirby knew making fuel purchases to the exact dollar, was not always easy. The apparent anomaly was Greg's log sheets always showed purchases of 39.99 litres, 44.99 litres or 61.99 litres etcetera, but never an even amount.

'Hey, what's with your fuel purchases always showing point 99 of a litre?' Kirby asked.

'Over the years I've run a few experiments to see just what the bureaucracy does with all the data they demand we give them. This is an ongoing experiment. Been doing it for ten years and no one from administration has ever passed comment. I just keep doing it now for the hell of it. Even if I say so myself I'm an expert at stopping fuel bowsers at point 99 of a litre.'

Some claim to fame Kirby thought as Greg continued.

'Another experiment relates to a long wheel base Isuzu utility we had here as a second vehicle. It was an absolute brute of a thing to drive. It gave me a stitch just driving along a good sealed road as it humped and bumped up and down so badly. Then we realised the benefits of a load in the rear. With a half-tonne of gravel in the back, that car was real good to drive. I thought log sheets should be used to work out fuel consumption and running costs etcetera, but apparently not. Our fuel consumption would have doubled after we started carting the extra half tonne of gravel around. But, again the bureaucracy in Melbourne didn't make a single comment.'

More claims to fame Kirby thought. Greg had not finished yet.

'At the top of all log sheets is a place to write the registered number and a considerable amount of other information about that specific vehicle. All this other information must be known from the registration number but for each page you have to clearly, accurately and legibly complete each of the boxes. For each and every log sheet I ever submitted for that vehicle I completed the space for "make and type" as, "Long wheel base no-can-bend-'em u beaut Isuzu ute." This was hardly accurate but again no one said a thing. Perhaps now you can see why I'm not a real fan of log sheets, journals, reports, requisitions, accounts and summaries. They don't add a darn thing to our work, or the department's efficiency for that matter. In fact I'm convinced the opposite is actually true.'

'What about other duties as directed?'

'Cheeky bugger. What about you get on with your other duties as directed?'

As Kirby returned to his relationship with FRED, he did see some merit in not having to duplicate so much superfluous information for the bureaucracy.

Chapter 2

In reality Greg had become bored and guilty sitting in the office while Kirby developed his rapport with FRED. The field trip they were now on had a bit to do with Greg's guilty conscience and the dirty office work he had left until Kirby arrived. From Kirby's perspective, he was now well aware being several hundred kilometres away from head office did not diminish any of FRED's capacity to dictate the political whim of the executive and bureaucracy. Everything, it seemed, was being done online these days.

So this was Kirby's first day out of the office at Mafeking Bay, doing real work! Work where a public servant managed without computers, fax machines and telephones. In today's progressive society, with all its advanced technology, work could violate even the most intimate personal functions, the mobile telephone the department issued to Kirby was waterproof!

Lincoln Campbell's licensed commercial fishing operations only allowed him to use a handful of rock lobster pots. Even with the high prices he received for the lobster he caught lawfully, Lincoln soon realised he wasn't going to make his fortune working like this. The answer to his financial worries had come to mind shortly after Greg Bayliss and Murray Stephens had prosecuted him for using too many rock lobster pots. Lincoln decided to supplement his income by diversifying. So, in addition to his licensed activities in the crayfish industry, Lincoln tried his hand at abalone poaching.

The two officers spent a few more minutes looking at the sign in the front yard and generally chatting about pirates who poach abalone. After a few minutes they drove away and purchased lunch at the café associated with the IGA supermarket. This was in a busy part of town, between the police station and the primary school, but there was always a place to park behind the supermarket. From there they went to the car park inside Rocklyn's Point. Here they overlooked the water in the direction of the sand dunes north of Point Alistree.

It was early November and quite hot for that time of year. Bass Strait was calm and the water sparkled silver-blue. Greg often came here to eat his lunch and today's choice of a spot for their break just happened without any forward planning.

A fishing boat or two moved in and out of the entrance. The view across to Point Alistree was quite spectacular. Kirby soon forgot FRED and was beginning to enjoy life as second in command at Mafeking Bay.

'This sure beats working for a living, don't you reckon?' Greg asked as he tucked into a bucket of chips and a coke. Kirby was not sure if Greg was referring to the seascape or his lunch. Greg's afterthought, 'Look at that for scenery!' only partially removed the confusion.

Kirby's lunch was not much better, a toasted ham and tomato sandwich with a carton of banana milk.

'It beats making eyes at FRED,' Kirby agreed. 'Tell me a bit more about Lincoln Campbell.'

'What do you know about abalone?' the boss challenged as though he had not heard the question. Kirby remembered Lincoln was a rock lobster fisherman, and although Greg had mentioned his abalone poaching, Kirby felt Greg was changing the subject. He found that a bit annoying.

'Some people believe it has aphrodisiac qualities. I tried 'em once and reckon they're worse to eat than old boot leather.'

'That's because they weren't cooked properly.'

Greg's opinion carried some weight as he was a member of the local beer, wine and cheese club. Rumour had it the menu for the club's annual dinners always contained abalone and Greg had always been the supplier. Rumour also suggested the source of the abalone was seized from poachers in the course of Greg's duties. Of course that was hearsay.

'Abalone has a divine flavour. I reckon it's a cross between lobster and scallops if they're done right. There's no doubt crook preparation or poor cooking, or both, can be a disaster. You treat them wrong and they're tough all right. It's all in the preparation. Good abalone's not tough, and it's definitely worth eating!'

'I'll have to get you to cook me some. What about Lincoln Campbell?'

'Abalone shell is mother of pearl,' Greg continued without even acknowledging Kirby's interest in the poacher. 'Sponges, algae and other marine growths are usually on the outside of their flat, brown shells. It's the inside that's got the beautiful pearl hues. When the ab fishery began in the 1960's prices were low and the real attraction was the sea and the lifestyle offered when you went fishing for a living. Today licence prices and fees reflect the fact abalone meat, not the shell, is very much in demand. That's why Lincoln's now into abalone poaching but he hasn't bothered about a licence. Wouldn't get one now anyway. Not with all his priors even if he had the millions required to buy one.'

Greg had hardly stopped to draw breath and now Kirby saw the subjects of abalone and Lincoln were linked, in Greg's view anyway.

'I remember, in 1972 or '73 I think it was, I was still pretty new in the job, when they introduced some new legislation. We called it the "shell law" and it was supposed to stop all fishermen taking undersize abalone by making them land it whole, and still in the shell. When the industry began they used to just land the meat with the shells being chucked back into the sea where they were caught. After this new law the abs had to stay in the shell all the way to the processing factory.

This was all supposed to help the State Government convince the Federal Government that Victoria was doing the right thing for sustainable development of our fishing industries. Look, if the industry had been fair dinkum they would have seen this as a good way to conserve stocks. If that had happened the feds wouldn't have been so gung-ho in relation to their political push for sustainable development.

'Anyway, the new shell law went over like a lead balloon with a few blokes in the industry. Most blokes actually, including all the divers here at the bay. One of my first ab jobs, with a team of others, was to do something about the problem. In a couple of days we'd booked the whole fleet for either shucking at sea or for landing shucked abalone, or both. You know what shucking means?'

'I might be green but I'm not a cabbage. It's just the removal of the abalone meat from its shell.'

'Yeah, all right. A few of them, the pro divers I mean, needed a couple of trips to court before they were convinced the department was serious about the shell law. One of them had a bit of a reputation, a bloke called Les Hoffmann. We had a Savage Marlin here as our patrol boat at the time. She was fitted with twin outboard motors. Les's boat could easily out-run it and he took great delight in playing games with us. As our boat approached he would haul his anchor and take off. As he sped away he pretended he did not know we were following. The noise of the motors on both boats, and water in his ears from diving, gave him a plausible excuse for not hearing our demands he stop.

'It was all great fun for Les, but when the department replaced the outboard motors on our boat with bigger ones, Les's reaction was simply. He just went out and traded his abalone workboat in on a nine metre ocean-racing hull. The department also changed its instructions to us officers who drove boats. They issued us all with a K Flag, the marine international signal flag for "Stop." It's yellow and blue. There's one on the boat if you want a look.'

Kirby did not want to look. He knew about the international signal flags. Greg did not miss a beat.

'This new boat was a beautiful iridescent purple, fitted with a monster V8 inboard motor and decked out to take abs. With his usual crew, but without bothering to register the new boat, Les just went off fishing. He steamed away from the bay, down towards the lighthouse. Darren Wossfold was my offsider in those days and we didn't have a clue about Les's new boat.

'Well anyway, this particular day was absolutely glorious, a bit hot mind you. Like today really. The sea was flat as. We were on patrol down the coast road in the car and there, a few bays back this way from the lighthouse, was this beast of a purple racing hull with no registration numbers.

'The boat raised our interest and we stopped for a bit of a squiz. Then I saw the gantry, fitted to the starboard side. Ocean racers don't need a gantry and that sure turned our attention away from the colour, size and shape of the hull. We had more than a casual interest now, and we began to do proper surveillance. Bugger me if there weren't two blokes in the boat, shucking abs and chucking the shells back in the sea.

'We had no camera. In those days the department didn't even know they'd invented cameras I don't think. We had no idea who the people in the boat were or where they'd launched. With a boat like that we even thought it could have travelled all the way from one of the ramps on the other side of Port Phillip Bay. We had no idea what to do.

'We were still procrastinating about our predicament when they hauled the anchor and the boat moved a bit closer to the lighthouse.

That was easy. We just followed along the coast road in the car. But it didn't get us anywhere really 'cos we knew we needed to intercept the boat but didn't know how. That was the hard bit.

'About half a kilometre or so short of the lighthouse the boat slowed and turned in towards the shore where it anchored again. It was less than fifty metres out and at that point the shoreline is just flat exposed reef that drops straight into three or four metres of water. It's a great place for a shore dive when the sea conditions are right.

'Then, bugger me, one of them, the bloke in the towelling hat, gets into a wetsuit and starts diving on hookah gear. The other bloke, the crew, helped him get geared up then continued shucking abs and chucking the shells back like before. Not long after this he looked like he'd done them all. He stopped tossing shells over and cleaned up the deck and sides of the boat.

'You wouldn't believe what happened then. He gets into a wet suit too and put on a SCUBA tank. We were positive we had ourselves an ab poaching operation of considerable proportions. Didn't keep an open mind, did we? Never thought it would have been an unlicensed bloke helping out a licensed diver. But had we thought that, we'd have been just as interested 'cos that's a real serious offence too. It amounts to unlicensed diving, just like any poaching.

'Anyway, I was pretty keen about catching these blokes and we hatched a plan that, in hindsight, was really a triumph of stupidity over good sense. It certainly didn't give much credence to occupational health and safety. But to be fair, OH&S wasn't really a consideration back then and neither were catch quotas for the ab industry.

'Darren was to stay in the car with his .270 Parker Hale rifle and I would swim out to the boat. With any luck we figured I could actually get into the boat while no one was aboard. If anything went wrong, Darren was a reasonable shot and the distance was pretty short. That was real smart, wasn't it?'

Greg did not really expect an answer. He continued without drawing breath.

'I got changed into my swimmers and tied an old metal ID badge onto the cord of my togs. I then swam out to the boat, making a detour out to sea to avoid swimming over the two sets of bubbles coming up. It was a pretty easy swim and I got aboard by using the dive ladder. I gave the thumbs up to Darren and had a bit of a gander round. There were two and a half bins of shucked abs and I just sat and waited, hiding in the cabin. Talk about luxury in a workboat!

'Guess who got back to the boat first?' Greg asked out of the blue.

'No idea. I wanted to know about Lincoln Campbell but you better finish this story now.'

'It was the deckhand,' Greg announced as if somehow this would make Kirby concentrate harder on the story he was telling. 'His heavy weight belt and SCUBA tank made it a bit hard for him to get back aboard, but I didn't help the bugger. He didn't know I was there, remember? Once he'd hauled himself up over the stern and flopped spread eagle on the deck I stepped quietly out of the cabin. Almost the instant he saw me he lunged to unsheathe a dive knife that was strapped around his calf.

'I still hadn't recognised him. At the same instant I yelled at him not to be stupid. I told him who I was and quickly added that Inspector Darren Wossfold was in the car watching us through the telescopic sight on a high-powered rifle. I waved at the shore where you could easy see our car.

'That must have given him more of a fright but he seemed to abandon the knife plan. I was pretty pleased about that but you wouldn't believe what happened then. It showed he got over his fright pretty quick.

'He knew I was an inspector because I'd met him previously but I still didn't know who either one of them were. I simply didn't recognise him because of the wet suit and wet hair and all. I asked who the diver was.

'He said, "It's Les."

'I had a good look at him then and with his face mask and wet suit hood off I could recognise him. It was Robert Grigg. We chatted for a bit about the new boat and he reckoned he was only looking for a crayfish and not taking abalone. I couldn't prove otherwise because he came back empty handed.

'Anyway, I gave him some strict instructions. I told him if he did anything to alert Les that I was on the boat when he got back he would be charged with obstruction. I told him the only trouble he was in at the moment was for shucking abs at sea. I explained that wasn't too serious, but an obstruction charge would put him into a different ball game, into the big league.

'He said he understood and I propped myself near the boat's windshield ready to duck into the cabin again, at the appropriate time. Ten minutes or so later Les appeared on the surface, near the stern of the boat. As all deckhands do, Grigg moved to help. As he reached over the side pretending to offer assistance he yelled out "The Fisheries are on board!"

'Les submerged like a crocodile, silently and completely. For the second time that day my enthusiasm, or stupidity, blocked out all thoughts of occupational health and safety. I jumped up and dived over the side following the bubbles and going as deep as I could. The white of the bubbles streaming to the surface showed me where to swim but I had no facemask and pretty soon ran out of puff. All I saw were the bubbles in a haze of bluish-green. My eyes were stinging from the salt water and I gave up and swam back to the boat.

'It was only then I thought how stupid I'd been. I hoped like crazy Darren would not, in all the confusion he must have seen, land a 270 slug into my brain as it broke the surface. Actually, as I climbed back on the boat I was wondering if I had any brains at all. Hell, maybe

I shouldn't have told you that story. Don't you ever do anything that stupid will you?'

Kirby was about to respond, trying to arrange his thoughts into a rational answer but he didn't have time.

'After a bit Les came back to the boat and Grigg winched up a net bag only about half full of abs. When he was back on the boat I didn't have time for an introduction. Les was a firm believer in the old adage, the best form of defence is attack.

'"Who the hell do you think you are?" he roared. "And what the hell are you doing on my boat?"

'I told him but he didn't give a rats. He just continued to give me a gob full. "Well I don't know who you are and unless you've got some form of official identification, you can get back into the water and swim from whence you've come."

'He said that you know, "from whence you've come," and I can still remember the exact words. I had no doubt he meant it too and would have physically chucked me off his boat. I also reckoned he was convinced I wouldn't be able to come up with any ID. There I was, dressed only in flimsy swimmers and without even a pen and paper!

'I showed him my old brass ID. We called them quandongs. Dunno where the name came from but I liked it. I was the last officer to ever be issued with one and I keep it at home now. It's a bit of a collector's item and if the boffins from head office ever remember I have one, I'll tell them it's lost. "Fisheries and Game Inspector" was embossed on one side and a crown and royal wreath on the other. Our new personalised photo identification cards are heaps better really.

'Anyway, Les accepted the quandong without a murmur and I had a bit of a gander at the abs that had just brought onto the boat. I wasn't surprised all of them looked real big and his catch-bag real empty considering the amount of time he'd been diving. Of course when he went back under water he knew I was there. I wonder what that was for, hey? Even if I had a measure with me, I wouldn't have needed to use it. Those abs were all well over the size limit, but I still had a job to do so I asked him for his abalone measure. You know the divers have to carry a measure when they're diving, don't you?'

'Err, yes,' Kirby spluttered.

'Wel, Les didn't have one and I'd decided to stitch him up for that, as well as breaking the shell law. It was about then I started to realise I was the one getting into trouble. Everything was getting a bit complicated for someone with no brains and no pen and paper to make notes with. I asked for his excuse for shucking abs at sea. In the circumstances I thought his explanation wasn't too bad for the spur of the moment.

'He said something along these lines. The shell law's bad for the industry. It's dangerous we have to carry three times more weight back after the day's fishing. That's why I've had to buy a bigger boat with a V8 motor. When we threw the gut and shells back into the water the spawn went back too. Making us land in the shell is going to destroy the stocks because there won't be any more spawning. This law will be the death of the industry. Could be the death of a diver too, or his deckhand or both. Like I said it's lots more dangerous carrying all the extra weight of the shell and the gut.

'Anyway, apart from that all being crap, I then knew who they both were, Les Hoffmann and Robert Grigg. This meant I didn't have to get their names and addresses. But there was a lot of detail I wasn't going to remember if I couldn't make some notes. I knew if I said anything about the unregistered boat I'd cop a gob full on that too. It'd be just be more detail I wouldn't be able to remember for court so I changed the subject.

'Great boat Les. How long have you had her?'

'First trip.'

'How does she go?'

'I was egging him on and I tried to sound interested but a bit off-hand at the same time, if you know what I mean.'

'Not bad.'

'I reckon he knew what I was up to and was just playing me along. Wouldn't mind a ride,' I said. 'What about taking me in to the lighthouse jetty?'

'Les just couldn't resist. He had to demonstrate the department would never have a boat as fast as his.

'"Yeah, no worries, pull the anchor," he said as he fired up big V8.

'I gave the thumbs up sign to Darren and pointed towards the lighthouse. Then I bloody near fell over backwards. The boat jumped up on the plane and with a hell of a roar, we took off.

'We were there well before Darren. Then he had to walk out from the car park. When he arrived, up on the jetty like he was and looking down into the boat, he could see the abalone meat too. Both of us could then give evidence we saw abalone meat on the boat at close range. That testimony would be hard to beat. Les was never going to get out of the shell law charge. Darren took some notes as I asked some more questions. That's how we wrapped up the case.'

'Wow,' said Kirby, trying to appear interested. 'What about you finish the story about Lincoln Campbell now?'

'I haven't finished this one yet,' Greg scolded. 'In those days the seizure provision under the 1968 Fisheries Act was only in relation to fish that were illegally taken. Those abalone were caught legally by a licensed diver. It was only after they were taken, and they were shucked, the law was broken. It was the possession, not the taking which was unlawful. We had no power to seize the fish and that was a real problem. I officially told Les the matters would be reported and the purple boat left in a haze of spray that drifted back to the jetty. There was a whiff of high octane fuel as well.

'Les did a bit of a circle around and past the end of the jetty and I reckon he wanted us to know he used high octane fuel just to rub in how fast he could go in his new toy. And I also reckon he deliberately did a big do-nut, swinging the boat away from the jetty just at the right moment to send an awesome spray up to wet me and Darren. Just as well it was a hot day, hey?'

'What about Lincoln Campbell?' Kirby quietly prompted again.

'Don't you want to know what happened in court?' Greg asked.

Kirby didn't really care but he knew he was going to find out.

'It was only after this case they amended the act,' Greg continued. 'And it was only when we could seize fish that were possessed unlawfully, as well as taken unlawful, that the divers started to get the message. Come hell or high water we intended to make the shell law work. Losing the days' catch was a pretty big punishment no matter what penalty the court handed out. Even Les didn't like being hit in the hip pocket.

'The fines from this particular court case certainly didn't worry Les too much. The magistrate dismissed the charge against Les, for allowing his crewman to dive during a commercial fishing operation. We proved everything except we couldn't prove Les knew his crewman was in the water. If he didn't know, how could he have allowed it? Remember the crewman left the boat after Les was underwater and he arrived back at the boat before Les did?

'Yes,' Kirby remembered grudgingly. He wanted to know about his new job and how Lincoln Campbell may influence his future work at Mafeking Bay. All Greg wanted was to keep Kirby's attention as it made him feel good telling war stories about himself.

'Hell, look at the time!' Greg interrupted Kirby's thoughts as he glanced at his watch. 'Lunch hour is well and truly over. We best get a move on or you won't learn a thing about this district. We've got a few things to see and you've got a few things to learn about this coast line.'

Greg backed out of the parking bay and drove off. As he did, Kirby decided to wait before he asked about Lincoln Campbell again. For a while there was silence as the two took in the scenery along the coast road towards the lighthouse. About ten kilometres down the road Greg suddenly pulled into a parking bay on a small headland. He parked at ninety degrees to the road. Kirby found himself overlooking a stretch of coast with a half moon bay to his left. A small creek entered the sea not far from the centre of the bay.

The tide was relatively low and the sand above the tide line was golden yellow. A couple walked along in the shallows holding hands and occasionally bending down to pick up shells. They huddled together obviously enjoying each other's company and the beauty of their newly found shell treasures. Two or three anglers were fishing from the rocks at the eastern end of the beach, directly in front of the car. It was so picturesque. Kirby smiled to himself, pleased with his move from head office.

Chapter 3

'This is a great place for shore based abalone poachers,' Greg announced, pointing to their right as he spoke. 'This little bay, and the area out front there, is all reef and relatively protected by the headland. Usually the experienced poachers get dropped off at this car park and they disappear down the access track before you can blink. It then takes three or four minutes for them to walk down to the bottom. From up here you can't see anyone or anything after they go over the edge and their drop off car has left.

'The poachers usually have a minder, a cockatoo, and he drives the car away so there's nothing to be seen if we come along at any time while they are poaching. The only window of opportunity is when they bring the abs back to the car. But it's only the dumb ones who do that when they first come back with their gear. It's all to show they are ready to leave but they always intend to return to get their bounty.

'If we want to do any good we have to counter their anti-surveillance tactics. If we stop here to look for signs down on the beach we simply let the cockatoo see us and then they make contact with the poachers via CB radio. Some of the more sophisticated operations now use mobile phones but they are pretty new and their coverage isn't too good in a lot of places.

'Actually, down the bottom of the track is a bit of a cliff and you can't see anyone at the base unless you walk right down. If you do though, you'll never get a case, except perhaps for a few innocent kids who don't know the law.'

'Where do the cockatoos keep their watch from?' Kirby asked. 'Surely we can come up with a scheme to out manoeuvre them?'

'That's exactly what we try to do. A good trick is for a male and female officer, pretending to be an item, to just front down and have a picnic near them, with a bit of a cuddle thrown in for authenticity. It's worked a couple of times with Darren Wossford and Jackie Blewitt the policewoman from Mafeking Bay. A few of the crews have woken up now which is a bit of a pity because Jackie is always pretty willing to help. She's is a bit of a sort too but it'd look a bit funny an old fart like me trying to pretend she was my girlfriend.'

'You might be her sugar daddy.'

'I wish. My best effort is to go down with another officer and start kicking a footy about. That's even a bit of a giggle really, me in shorts and thongs with my belly and lily-whites. The good poaching crews just don't trust anyone. A couple canoodling on the sand is about the only way to get close. You and Jackie might get a case with a bit of luck. Mind you, you'd better behave; she's a karate instructor and can look after herself when it matters.'

'That might be a bit academic. I can't see Nicky agreeing to it.'

'Obviously a government car, binoculars, radios and all our normal gear give the game away,' Greg continued without acknowledging Kirby's concern. 'Wearing work boots with plain clothes has even brought us undone. Our work boots have a distinctive sole pattern and those fresh footprints in the sand are like putting an announcement over a loud hailer.

'Another thing we do is try to use their tactics. That works sometimes. We get dropped off before daylight and hide where we think they might go poaching. If we're in there when the poachers arrive, and if we see them dive through the telephoto camera lens, we're in with a chance. It sure gives them a shock when they see the photos later. We often get them in the nuddy when they get changed into their wet suits. That sometimes makes them plead guilty. Don't like their nude photos being tendered in court I suppose. Come on I'll show you.'

Greg led the way down the track right to the beach. He pointed out a couple of good vantage points, warning at the same time a good spot to sit and watch was as good for the poacher's cockatoo as it was for an inspector.

When they reached the small cliff at the bottom of the track Greg suddenly stopped walking and turned to face Kirby. The moment he opened his mouth Kirby knew he was about to hear another war story. There was nothing more said about the shore dives Kirby thought they had come down the track to discuss.

'You know,' Greg started and then momentarily stopped as if gathering his thoughts. 'We did get an abalone pinch from here once but it was sort of boat and shore based at the same time. They used a rubber ducky launched over the beach a couple of bays back and then dropped two SCUBA divers here. Then the boat left with one bloke aboard and he went back to the bay were they had launched from. Here he put two new tanks in the boat and exactly an hour later was back where he had dropped the divers.

'We got a tip off and worked out their modus operandi. We figured out the one hour bit related to how long the divers could last underwater on one scuba tank. To bust them we seized the boat and arrested the driver when he came back to get the next two tanks. Then we seized his hat and coat and I put these on and drove back to give the divers their new tanks. They were out a bit from the shore but were still clearly visible from the car park where we had arranged for a couple of cops to arrive at exactly the right time. Surprise, surprise! I flashed my ID and indicated the police car that was now at the top of the track with its lights flashing. That wouldn't have worked with Lincoln Campbell and some of the real pirates, but it worked on them. They just gave up.'

Fifteen minutes later Kirby and Greg were back in the car, driving the coast road towards the lighthouse again. The senior officer then continued the Lincoln Campbell saga as if there had been no interruption.

'I remember the first time I ever booked Lincoln was just after we got the new Shark Cat to replace the old patrol boat. I was with Darren Wossfold and we were counting and inspecting crayfish pots. You've guessed it, we were after Lincoln because of all the complaints about him over-potting. Using more gear than his licence allowed, you know? From our perspective checking actual numbers of cray pots is three tasks really. Firstly you have to count each buoy and then cross reference your counts with the numbers of pots on the licence. But counting and cross referencing is pretty useless if that's all you do because it doesn't tell you what's on the end of the rope attached to the buoys. No, you have to know about the number of pots being used, not the number of buoys in the water. In court the argument would be the buoys marked the location of a cave or a shipwreck or anything except a pot. So the next job was to prove the number of buoys equalled the number of rock-lobster pots. Then this evidence has to be related to the number of pots the licence specifically allows the particular fisherman to use.

'It was another great day, bright and sunny and the water was clear. There was a reasonable swell running but the waves were round and gentle, only standing up close to shore. Some of the gear we inspected was in relatively shallow water and we could actually see two or three pots on the bottom.

'We did a quick scout around all the buoys we could see. All but two had Lincoln's numbers on them and there were about half a dozen over his entitlement. The unmarked ones we just hauled and kept aboard. These had fresh bait in them so we knew he'd already done his rounds that morning.

'We still had to determine if all the marked floats had pots attached. We started to do this. I kept the notes and Darren hand hauled the ropes until the pot was visible. To prevent double counting we tied a small plastic ribbon around the buoy before letting the pot drop back to the bottom. We'd finished five or six when I saw an open runabout coming up on us real quick from the beach.

'"Don't look now," I said to Darren. "We're about to be boarded and I think I know who the pirate is." It was Lincoln all right and his intentions were pretty clear. What we were doing was perfectly legal but that didn't interest him. All he wanted to do was to stop our investigation into his fishing activities. To demonstrate his resolve Lincoln had an axe! He steamed up hurling abuse, a bit like a pirate attack with an axe instead of a cutlass. He intended boarding our boat whether it was legal or not!

'As he got closer I thought he'd chuck the axe at us. It didn't take long for him to convince me either our boat, or Darren or I, would soon require urgent reconstruction or medical attention. We had no fibreglass repair kit and the Band-Aids in our first aid box seemed way too small for an axe wound. I'm not sure if it was the inadequacies of our first aid kit, my hatred of blood or the wild stories about Lincoln, but I pretty soon had nothing on my mind except our occupational health and safety. In all the circumstances I decided it was best to respect Lincoln's wishes for once. We steamed off in a bit of a hurry, headed towards Tasmania.

'Lincoln's boat was an open, aluminium run-about, about five metres long. Along both sides where normal people would put the boat's name, Lincoln had a stencil of a skull and crossbones. I often wondered why he didn't fly a Jolly Roger in his yard instead of the Southern Cross. I guess his passion for the dinkum Aussie battler and the Eureka Stockade have remained his real obsession. Trouble is, Lincoln fervently believed when he broke our fisheries laws, his actions were as legitimate as the miner's revolt against an oppressive Colonial Government in 1854.

'Anyway, Lincoln's boat had tiller-controls on a twenty-five or thirty horse power outboard. She had a fair turn of speed and as I motored off, Lincoln chased us. We left him behind pretty quick because the Shark Cat's got monster motors and we easily accelerated away. I stopped and Darren used the radio to report to head office. He told them a hostile boarding party was attempting to pirate our boat but we were taking positive, evasive action. That caused a bit of a stir I can tell you. All they wanted was an immediate explanation but we couldn't give them one.

'Lincoln had just about caught up by now and he was hopping mad, I can tell you! I had to get out of the way and I drove off again, flat out and still going south. The further from the coast we went the bigger the swells got. They were not huge dangerous swells, just large round hills of water. Our cat and mouse game continued for a fair while. We would stop to use the radio and Lincoln, still mad as a hatter, would steam up closer and closer. It was pretty darn clear his anger was getting worse and worse. He didn't give a hoot we were now miles from his fishing equipment.

'In retrospect I wonder if we didn't incite Lincoln because he thought we were deliberately baiting or tormenting him. He could have thought, initially anyway, when we were stopped he would be able to move in for the coup de grâce. In reality we had to stop to use the radio because, so far from the base, the boat radio was all static from electrical interference from the out-board motors. We needed to switch them off to make audible contact with the office. Anyway it doesn't matter now.

'I can tell you the boffins in head office got into a real tizz when they found out what was really going on. Of course they only got a bit of the picture at the time then had to wait five minutes or so for the next epistle. Pretty soon the prospect of a massive hike in next year's personal liability insurance premiums was causing all sorts of coronaries with the bean counters in head office!

'Anyway, we started and stopped a few more times. By now everyone was real frustrated. Our boat was so large compared to Lincoln's and we hadn't done anything wrong, like I said. It was as if Lincoln was in a trance, crouched up on the rear seat and still working the tiller with his left hand. He was just a crazy man, real mad. He continually shouted obscenities at us across the water and all the time was holding the axe in his right hand and waving it at us every time he thought we were looking at him. Hell, I can tell you the thought of the paperwork associated with that little episode was enough for me.'

'Yeah,' said Kirby thinking of the amount of paperwork he had inherited and had to wade through since coming to Mafeking Bay. 'I can relate to that. What happened? How did the whole thing end up?'

'Well,' Greg mused, rubbing his chin, 'for a while there I contemplated letting Lincoln get close enough to chuck the axe, sort of a catalyst to put a stop to it all. I thought then we might've been able to interview him and finalise the whole stupid affair. But being a real mental giant, I soon realised this was not a good punt; it lacked a degree of control on my part. Lincoln had the axe and I didn't have the guts to give it a try!

'We were now so far south you couldn't see Australia except from the top of the biggest swells. Like I said the swells were large round hills of water and they gave us a fantastic roller coaster ride in the Shark Cat, provided we didn't hit them head on, at ninety degrees and flat out. The cat's a real heavy boat and when she lands back in the water after shooting off the crests, you know all about it, I can tell you.

'There were a few times Lincoln's boat did just that you know. It flew clean off the top of a wave. Completely airborne it was.

Under his boat I could even see the propeller out of the water. Hell it was a sight! At the same time I could see Lincoln, still waving the axe and crouched on the rear seat. I can still see it plain as day. I reckon Walt Disney would have been proud of it in a Yosemite Sam cartoon!

'We radioed the office and arranged for the cops to meet us at the boat ramp. After this was all fixed up, we headed off and left Lincoln with the albatross, storm petrels and Great White Sharks. The swells were now on our stern and we went like a rocket. That trip was great.

'The police were waiting at the ramp back in Mafeking Bay and we tied up the boat and got in the police car. On the way we gave the boys in blue all the details of what happened. Well, Jackie was there so it was the boy and girl in blue. We went to the station first and made written statements for them. After an hour or so, when we finished the paperwork and had a cuppa, we headed off to Lincoln's place.

'Lincoln answered the door and that was the first we knew he got back safely. Then, just like everyone should have guessed, Lincoln gave us a real warm and friendly greeting. He was obviously pretty pleased to see us.

'"What do youse bastards want?" he yelled.

'The sergeant told him the police needed to ask some questions about the incident with the axe in the boat.

'"Axe, what axe?" Lincoln interrupted. "I don't even own an axe."

'I suppose we didn't expect him to, but Lincoln didn't admit a thing. Anyway the police didn't worry too much about lack of admissions and eventually the summons invited Lincoln to court. He defended himself and when the evidence was over the court gave him a lecture about not believing his story. The magistrate really got stuck in. He said what Lincoln did that day was totally unacceptable; "the actions of a savage, a primitive cave man," I think were his words. We reckoned it just proved Lincoln really was a pirate.

'"Society expects the legal system to support officers acting in the course of their duties" the magistrate went on to say. "After all they act on behalf of the whole community looking after our valuable fishing industry, the fish resources and the natural environment. It is the court's job today to fulfil the needs and expectations of the majority of people. In fact, I am considering sending you to prison. Do you wish to say anything about that?"'

Greg suddenly stopped the car again.

'This is where we first saw Les's purple abalone boat,' he announced. 'See, you can see the lighthouse from here.'

Kirby looked in the direction Greg pointed and about two thirds of the lighthouse stood tall above the tree-lined hills of the national park. The sun was still high in the sky but a thick bank of grey clouds had appeared out to sea. From where the officers sat it seemed as though the clouds were directly above the lighthouse. That could not be so because the beacon sparkled in bright sunlight. To the south, from the horizon to the inner edge of the clouds, the water was royal blue, almost purple. Closer to shore the water varied from an attractive aqua to various shades of green and grey-blue. There was a clear line between the darker, distant colours and those in the foreground. Kirby looked with delight at the picturesque setting that was now his workplace. The dazzling white of a wave breaking on a reef contrasted with the rest of the seascape.

'This is a pretty good place for abalone too but there is nowhere for the poachers to hide here,' Greg announced, his words interrupting Kirby's thoughts. 'They're supposed to dive here at night a bit during real good weather but you don't get too many big cases from this spot. A fair few divers come here after crays, more than abs I'd reckon.'

'What about re-breathers for SCUBA divers after abs?' Kirby asked. 'If they used re-breathers they could poach abs here all day right under our noses. They could leave the abs in a gutter close in to shore somewhere and come out of the water and back to their car carrying nothing. They could then come back after dark to pick up the fish. That would be a pretty good ploy, especially if they carried an underwater camera as a decoy in case we saw them initially come ashore.'

Greg put the car into gear and moved off, deliberately not acknowledging Kirby's astute appraisal of the situation or his implied question. Without hesitation the senior man continued his story about Lincoln and the axe. Kirby guessed Greg either did not know how a re-breather worked or was just being sanctimonious because he had the floor, as it were.

'Back to the court case,' Greg said. 'After the magistrate told Lincoln he was considering putting him away, I didn't think Lincoln would say anything. But he did. He moved from where he was behind the bar table and walked forward three of four steps, right up to the dais. The height to the top of the magistrate's bench was about the same height as the top of Lincoln's head. He placed his hands up and hung on, pulling himself up so he could see the magistrate, eyeball to eyeball. From where the magistrate sat I reckon Lincoln would have looked like Foo peering over a wall. Anyway, hanging in that position, Lincoln gave the magistrate a real gob full.

'"There's nothing you can do to frighten me," he said.

'Lincoln's words were driven through clenched teeth as if he was speaking past a cutlass held tightly in his mouth. Lincoln was facing away from me at the time but everyone in the court heard and understood. He sure wasn't frightened by the magistrate. Several cops rushed up and we had the makings of a second Mutiny on the Bounty. Luckily Lincoln was back on the floor pretty quick and it was all over without any real violence.

'Darren and I reckoned our ordeal in the boat with Lincoln waving the axe was worth a stint in clink by itself. By the time Lincoln finished his antics in the courtroom, we would have taken all bets he was off the jail for a very long stint. We were right. The court put Lincoln in for three months but he immediately appealed and walked out on bail.

'When the appeal came up, the judge allowed the appeal and ordered Lincoln's term of imprisonment be served at an attendance centre, not actually in jail. All that meant was Lincoln had to spend working hours at the centre as a prisoner. A bit like Rene Rivkin except Lincoln was allowed home at night and on weekends. Renee had to spend his weekends in the lock up. It saves the government money if they don't keep prisoners in full time. Just think of the savings alone if they don't have to provide meals!

'Anyway, it didn't take too long and a new sign sprang up in Lincoln's yard. The new one looked like it was painted with a thumbnail dipped in tar, just like the one we saw earlier. I wish I'd taken a photo of it. It didn't stay up long but it said something like "No crayfish due to the illegal seizure of a professional fisherman's crayfish pots. An act of piracy at sea in defiance of the High Court of Australia."

'The high court bit was a reference to a case where the court had ruled the seizure of some gear by a Commonwealth Fisheries Officer was not legal because the officer had not shown his authority and his ID badge to the boat's skipper when he boarded. That's a legal requirement of the Commonwealth Fisheries Management Act but it has got no bearing whatsoever on our seizure of Lincoln's pots under the Victorian one. A mere legal technicality like that didn't worry Lincoln though.

'Anyway, back to the story. As you know, Lincoln doesn't live right in Mafeking Bay, sort of on the outskirts and the attendance centre is in Costerfield. That's a fair old drive there and back each day. On the first morning he was driving in and the cops got him for driving when his licence was cancelled. He ended up doing time on that charge. Actually it was three months in the end so he was inside for exactly the same time as the original sentence.'

'I think I can see why Lincoln might have a dirty on,' Kirby observed.

'What's the score about us inspecting his pots without the police being there?' Kirby asked, raising OH&S questions without actually saying all he thought. 'The manual has a bit to say on potentially dangerous situations.'

'Yes, you must always get the police,' Greg warned. 'There is also a written instruction from Murray Stephens specifically about Lincoln Campbell. It's in the office. We have to let head office know any time we intend to work him, and we have to have direct communications with the police station as well as having a police member with us. But you know, apart from him being a big time abalone poacher now, Lincoln does have a bit of a sense of humour. There's a fair bit more to him than you see on face value.'

'Well, tell me,' Kirby invited. 'I can't believe this bloke. What else does he do?'

'A fair bit I suppose. To start with he stopped submitting his monthly fish returns. When he did the three months inside, nobody bothered to tell the department's catch and effort section he wouldn't be fishing for a while. They sent him three letters about late returns, one for each month he was in jail. Then, when Lincoln got out the reminder letters bounced like rubber cheques. Lincoln sent them all back with some friendly words of advice written all over them.

'The catch and effort section sent me copies with a note that said, "Please stop annoying our conscientious fishermen." I've kept the copies. Remind me to show you one day when we're in the office. They're pretty funny really.

'One of Lincoln's little gems said something about not fishing due to harassment from the government. If I remember right, it said, "Please refrain from sending me these notices all the time. I do not work for the government. If you wish to assess what's in the sea, I suggest your department employs fisheries inspectors and their boats to do this instead of such boats harassing fishermen." He signed it "Captain Lincoln Campbell." He drew a skull and cross-bones on this just like he does with everything he signs.

'I reckon prison taught him a thing or two 'cos not long after he got out he tried to secede from the Commonwealth of Australia. He must have struck some legal loophole though because the tax-man and local council refused to recognise his sovereign state. Remind me to tell you about it some time.'

'He sure is a character,' Kirby observed.

'Yes,' said Greg. 'As well as thinking he is above the law he has a reputation based on some rather scary stories. On more than one occasion the local cops had to call for reinforcements when they were breaking up one of Lincoln's pub brawls. One time one of his victims spent several months in hospital before the police prose-cution could get off the ground. There's no doubt Lincoln flies his Eureka Flag with a great deal of passion. He hates politics and the bureaucracy. I think his use of the skull and crossbones is sheer dev-ilment. He wants everyone to know if they cross him they should expect to be in for a fight. He's been to jail about his fishing returns too, you know.'

Kirby did not know.

'You've seen the return forms haven't you?' Greg asked. 'You know they ask for all this data to be completed in a hundred differ-ent boxes. The names of crew, the dates fished, the number of the boat, the type of gear, the time spent fishing, the time spent search-ing, the species caught, how many and where they were sold and so on and so forth.

'The department says it has tried to make the form as easy as pos-sible and they provide all the paperwork, folders, prepaid envelopes and sheets of carbon paper etcetera. After all the trouble they go to, the bureaucracy just won't accept excuses for failure to send in monthly returns. They say it costs the fisherman nothing except a few minutes time each month and there are heaps of spares in their folder if they muck one up. The old excuse, "it must have got lost in the post," just doesn't wash any more. The department says, "Pop the carbon copy in the mail and no worries." Trouble is, mostly the fishermen don't use the carbon paper or if they do, they put it in upside down or something.

'Look, let's be honest. Lots of fishermen don't see fish returns in quite the same light as the department's boffins, bean counters and scientists. Some have genuine difficulty filling in the forms. Lots of them, like Lincoln, don't see the need to tell the department anything.

A bit like you and your log sheets, journals, reports, requisitions, accounts and summaries, thought Kirby as Greg continued.

'Some are a bit scared the taxman may find out something they don't want him to know. Others object because the department does nothing constructive with the data. Heaps of them took up fishing as a job because they liked the outdoor lifestyle. Paperwork, figures and politics are bulldust as far as they are concerned. They reckon all that should be left to accountants, public servants and politicians.

'You can probably imagine Lincoln isn't particularly good at submitting clear, legible, true and accurate returns. His spelling sometimes lets him down in the accuracy and legibility departments but that's not the real problem. The information he provides usually isn't true because it has nothing to do with fishing. He insists the information requested is confidential and none of the department's business. According to him the department needs to get its act together first. He says the lack of his correct title on the pre-printed forms actually offends him. Lincoln always crossed out L Campbell and replaced it with "Captain Lincoln Campbell" and the little picture of his beloved skull and crossbones.

'On one return he drew a large picture of a whale and a stick-figure shaking a fist under a schwasticker. He filled in his crew as "Harpee and Yippe" and most of his comments were X-rated for sure.

'His comments are funny really, if you're not too prudish. Eventually though the aggressive lack of harmony between the bureaucracy and Lincoln meant I had to go and interview him about his monthly fish returns, or lack of them really. I took the police of course. Lincoln was simply unrepentant. He'd had dozens and dozens of reminder letters.

'This is the case I was telling you about. The one where Lincoln got sent to jail because of his refusal to put in fish returns. When the case came on, Lincoln didn't appear and we gave the evidence without him. The magistrate just convicted him and fined him a couple or three hundred bucks or something. I forget the detail but that doesn't matter.

'Anyway, we had a few cases on that day and I was giving evidence in the next one when I saw Lincoln walk into the courtroom. When I finished, I told the magistrate the defendant in the previous matter had just arrived.

'The magistrate fired a few questions at Lincoln about being late. I could see his blood pressure rising and I thought he was going to pop again, but he didn't. Eventually the court agreed to re-hear his case and we gave the evidence for a second time. That was a bit of an experience you know, getting the story to sound the same two times in about ten minutes.

'Anyway at the end of my evidence the magistrate asked Lincoln if he agreed he had not put his returns in. Lincoln admitted he hadn't and explained he hadn't been fishing. He then tried to give the magistrate a lecture on the inappropriateness of the law and the unethical way the department sought to obtain confidential business information. Now it was the magistrate's turn to have a coronary.

I could see his blood pressure shooting through the roof too. I was surprised how long he let Lincoln prattle on.

'Lincoln eventually finished and the magistrate said, "I see no reason why my original penalty should be altered. Convicted and fined four hundred dollars," or whatever it was. Lincoln turned and started walking towards the door. Then he stopped and turned to face the magistrate again. He looked straight at him and let him have it.

'"Thanks very bloody much, you great fat fart," he said to the magistrate.

'Everyone in the court nearly dropped dead but Lincoln wasn't finished yet. "What should I expect? You're just a bloody public servant like the rest of them. You work for the government and they pay you. I should have bloody known you'd just do what they want."

'Well, that was that. The magistrate really flipped. He demanded the police on the door arrest Lincoln for contempt. "Take him over to the station and leave him in the cells till I've finished the list. We'll get him back here then when he has no audience to play up to. Perhaps a few hours in the cell will help him realise he can't behave like that in my court. Contempt in this court will be punished by imprisonment!"

'And that's what happened. Lincoln went to jail because he didn't put in fish returns. I think it's a bit of a record really. No other inspector I know has had a case of going to jail for no fish returns. And on top of that, Lincoln wasn't fishing for those months anyway.'

'Hardly a record to be proud of. It was his contempt of court and not his lack of returns, or even his scornful attitude towards the authority of the department, that put him in jail.'

'Same thing really,' Greg stated flatly. 'Lincoln just hates anyone telling him what's what and what he's got to do and what he's not allowed to do. But they tell me he's on medication now to control his anger. The police say it's working too. He hardly goes to the pub anymore and if he does, he drinks light and they don't have any trouble with him. He's still into abalone poaching though. Like the rest of us he is getting older and has to be slowing down. You'd think he must have learnt a thing or two about behaving after all his trips to court too. I remember the first time I saw him in court,' and Greg was off telling another war story.

Chapter 4

'Remember I told you Lincoln had two brothers, Michael and Bernard? Well, the first time I saw Lincoln in court he wasn't even a defendant. I'd booked Michael and Bernard and was sitting in court waiting for their case to be called. In those days we used to have court at Mafeking Bay but it was held in the public hall that was specifically set up for court once a month. We only ever had court 12 times a year, but now all our cases go to Costerfield and they are held in the proper court house every fortnight.

'Back then though, two trestle tables represented the magistrate's bench and the bar table. The devised court chamber included a table for the clerk of courts, chairs for the officials and a few seats behind the bar table. These few seats did not substitute for the public gallery but allowed solicitors to have their clients seated close by during the actual case. Members of the public and people waiting for their cases to be called could not sit close enough to hear the proceedings.

'At the rear of the hall were six or eight rows of cinema seats and behind these on the wall was a picture of a very young Queen Elizabeth II. The seats here were on a section of the floor that sloped slightly upwards towards the back, obviously the back picture stalls in days gone by. Between there and the stage was a large ballroom and the distance between this public gallery and the front of the make-shift court room was considerable.

'Immediately our case was called, I made application for a joint hearing as the second brother's case arose from the same set of circumstances. When the clerk of courts called the two names, three men walked from the stalls.

'The three brothers crossed the expanse of wilderness and walked the length of the ballroom towards the make-shift bench and bar table. There was an air of expectancy as Lincoln was wearing thongs and a tee shirt. The stars of the Southern Cross proudly displayed on his back and the words "Free Australia" called out from the front of his shirt.'

'"Which one of you is Michael Campbell?" the magistrate asked.

'"That's me," said Michael.

'"And which is Bernard Campbell?" continued the magistrate.

'"That's me," answered Bernard.

The magistrate looked at the third person. '"And who are you?"

'"I'm Lincoln, their big brother. I'm their legal adviser," he said confidently.

'"Are you a qualified lawyer?" The court did not really need an answer to this question.

'"No, but me brothers don't talk proper, so I'm here to help 'em out."

'Lincoln was absolutely serious; he had been in court many times and knew the ropes. Somehow these previous cases failed to convey the relevance of the magistrate's question. To be permitted to practise law in Victoria one must hold an appropriate qualification. The same is true of medicine, plumbing and a host of other occupations.

'"Well, you go back and sit where you were. Afterwards, if the defendants so desire, and you have some relevant evidence that can be given from personal knowledge, you will be given the opportunity to speak."

'Lincoln slowly trudged back to his seat at the rear of the hall.'

Greg stopped the car again, this time in the car park near the gate in the fence around the lighthouse grounds. There were two other cars in the park and one was a police car.

'Come and have a look at this. The lighthouse is all automated now and there is no lighthouse keeper as such. The place has been taken over by national parks and it's really just a tourist attraction these days. We should be able to get a cook's tour with a bit of luck. Mellissa Elliot is the officer stationed here and she's a good scout. I hear tell there's a local nudist club and she's one of the leading lights. That's all hearsay by the way, and if you ask her about it, I'll dong you. Seriously, she often gives us a ring about what she sees and hears. She's a real good contact down here for what's going on in the poaching world. I'll introduce you.'

The lighthouse keeper's cottage had been converted to a small museum that was open to the public. Kirby guessed the museum was now in what had been the dining or sitting room and off this, in what was previously the kitchen, was a small office and tea room for staff. Here the fisheries officers found Mellissa talking to a police woman. Greg obviously knew both and made the introductions. The police woman was Jackie Blewitt.

During the small talk, Mellissa locked the door and made coffee for everyone. While having their cuppa the conversation got around to their respective law enforcement roles in the district. Mellissa's work in the rescue of sick, injured or orphaned animals seemed to hold the most interest. She was as good, or perhaps even better, than Greg at war stories.

'Greg, you will remember last year,' Mellissa said. 'The press and TV gave a fair bit of coverage to an oil spill off the coastline of our national park. We were both involved in the aftermath of the spill and while our spill wasn't as bad as when the Exxon Valdez spilled eleven million gallons of oil into Prince William Sound, it was bad enough. I think the EPA is still prosecuting the company and the ship's captain over our spill. They collected oil samples from along our coast line and compared the chemical composition to the oil in various ships that went through Bass Straight in the week or so before the spill. That's all very scientific and a bit out of my league I'm afraid, but I do hope they get what they deserve in court.

'For the first few days after the pollution started coming ashore there were oiled sea birds everywhere. There were hundreds of fairy penguins because of the rookery on Mafeking Island. There were lots of mutton birds, cormorants, prions and gulls and a few albatross as well. Most were dead or died soon after we collected them. From stress associated with being handled by humans as well as ingestion of the oil as they tried to preen their feathers.

'The clean up on the beaches was bad enough but it was impossible along the rugged and rocky cliff areas so there was an ongoing problem with the pollution and the oiled sea birds. It lasted for weeks really. Long term and obscure consequences must still be there I suppose. Will be for years, don't you think? I reckon we have no real understand of the enduring problems for our ecosystems from such a disaster.

'Along the inaccessible places we just had to let nature do her thing but along the beaches we did regular patrols picking up the stragglers we found. It was very time consuming but good exercise. As I was doing those patrols I often thought; all this and I'm getting paid to do it too. I know I am lucky to have such a good job. Sometimes though, when I am working out-doors in the pouring rain or freezing cold, I have to remind myself of the good days. On days when the weather is perfect it makes up for a lot I reckon.

'Near the end of the whole oil spill saga the weather was perfect. It was warm and sunny. There wasn't a cloud in the sky, there was no wind and the forecast was for continued fine weather. The public interest in the seabirds, even the penguins, had dropped right off and it was the middle of the week. I got the job of the last foot patrol of Five Mile Beach. It's a pretty remote beach but easy to get to by boat. That's what I did this day, went by boat. I remember the sea was so calm. It was glassy. It was simply beautiful.

'When I got there, the tide was still dropping. I put out a stern anchor and pulled the bow right in to the beach. I knew as the tide dropped the boat would be stranded, but it didn't matter. With a bow anchor right up the beach I knew the boat would be safe, and I calculated it would be floating again by the time I finished the walk from that end of the beach to the other and back.

'Look, you probably know this from the gossip around town but that beach is used a bit by nudists. There was no one about and it was a perfect day so I decided to do my patrol in the all-together. I took a back pack with supplies and set off, wearing my hat.

'I didn't see a single soul all the way there but when I was about two thirds of the way back, I could see another boat close in to where I'd left my boat. I didn't know if they were there to pinch something or if my moorings had failed and they were there saving the boat from being wrecked. I didn't know whether to run or to hide.

'The worst thing was my boat had "NATIONAL PARKS" written down both sides. I was worried these people might dob me in. They would obviously be able to read and I was wearing my uniform hat that showed where I worked too.'

Kirby thought about asking Mellissa if she had found any oiled penguins but kept his mouth shut, more than a little embarrassed. Jackie didn't say a word either, and for once, Greg was also silent.

'To hell with it I thought.' Mellissa continued not the least embarrassed telling her story. 'I might as well get it over with. I just kept walking as if the other boat wasn't there. Pretty soon I could see the other boat had writing down the side too. You wouldn't believe it but it was the water police from Melbourne!

'Now I started to think they might arrest me and what that would do for my job. Pretty soon though I figured they would have checked me out with binoculars by then and nothing I could do was going to change a thing. I just walked on right back to the boat.

'Sorry Jackie but those cops were just disagreeable, mongrel, low lives. They had checked me out and they were just waiting there to see what I would do. I guess they originally expected me to change before I got back to the boat. They would have thought I had clothes in the back pack but I didn't. I only had water and bags and gear for the oiled penguins. They took great delight in gawking as I waded out to the boat and climbed back aboard. As I got to the boat, I simply said, "Nice day fellas, can I help you with something?"

'I won't tell you what one of them said but you can imagine. I went into the cabin, put on my shorts and shirt. I just pulled the anchors and took off without saying another thing to them. They followed for half a mile or so, then did a one-eighty and headed back the other way.'

It was about 7:30 pm when the officers arrived back at the office.

Chapter 5

With the opening of the crayfish season still a few days away, Lincoln's cash flow was anything but healthy. During the first couple of weeks of the open season the sale price for crayfish was usually very good, but the South Australian season opened before the Victorian one. Lincoln was always annoyed at the government over this. Like many fishermen, he reasoned the premium prices paid by the patrons of the Melbourne Spring Racing Carnival, should be lining his pockets.

These bonanza prices were falling by the time the Victorian fish came on the market. Lincoln was aware that one of the purposes of the Victorian Fisheries Act was "to ensure the welfare of the fishing industry and those engaged in it." He reasoned the department should be prosecuted for dereliction of its duty. He had never seen them looking after the people engaged in the fishing industry.

Lincoln was desperate for money just to pay the regular household bills, despite him having worked at Bowtell's Boat Yard on and off for years. Bernie Bowtell, a local boat dealer, also did boat repairs and service. He gave Lincoln work off and on, especially during the winter off-season.

For several weeks before the crayfish season opened, Lincoln had been involved in several long conversations with Bernie. They had committed themselves to a new venture. Lincoln's forward planning involved less and less reliance on catching crayfish for a living because, he argued to himself, this new venture was forced upon him by an incompetent government and inept fisheries managers. All they were interested in was politics and they didn't care about the welfare of the fishing industry or the people engaged in it. If they did, the Victorian season would open before the South Australian one and he would receive better prices for his early season crayfish.

Lincoln knew if he took his cray-fishing boat to sea before the season opened he would arouse the suspicion of the other fishers from the bay. If they spilled the beans the chances of him being detected rose sharply. In an attempt to neutralize this potential problem, Lincoln made sure several of the locals knew he was going out to do sea trials as part of his work with the boat builder. His co-conspirator in the plan was the proprietor of the boat business himself.

Bernie and Lincoln discussed which boat to borrow for their operation. There were two possibilities in the yard at the time. The first was a Shark Cat that had the windscreen, seats and transom removed as part of its rebuild. The second was a small Haines Hunter fitted with a single, large outboard. It too, had no windshield.

'The Shark Cat is owned by a licensed abalone diver from Melbourne,' Bernie said. 'He has two boats and leaves this one here with me in storage and only uses it a couple of times a year. It's all just a tax dodge. He comes down here on holidays but goes professionally diving once during the month and claims the whole trip as a work related tax deduction. We should take the cat I reckon. The owner will never find out. He knows he can't use it during the repairs and he never comes down at this time of the year anyway. I told him I wouldn't have it ready for a couple of weeks yet. He always has his holidays at Christmas and in January then comes down again at Easter. I'll have it ready by then.'

'That's great,' Lincoln agreed. 'The way she is set up has some excellent design features too if there is a need for us to expeditiously and unobtrusively jettison anything. Over my years in the fishing industry I've encountered this need on more than one occasion you know.'

Bernie laughed. 'I bet you have.'

'We have to do internal hull inspections as part of the boat's rebuild, don't we?' Lincoln asked.

'Yep. Why?'

'Well,' mused Lincoln. 'If we cut through the floor into the respective pontoons we could use the holes to stand in, one for the driver and one for the passenger. We can put a make shift floor in the pontoons if necessary. When we're travelling, our profile will be very low and we'll be pretty hard to see.'

'The Marine Board might have a bit of a fit if they see us,' Bernie observed. 'Also could be a bit dangerous if we hit any rough water. Shark Cats are self-draining and I like safety in the design of a boat. These modifications will neutralize the self-draining capacity.'

'Don't be such a bloody sissy,' Lincoln responded. 'Do you want to make a quid or not? Besides tomorrow's weather forecast is good and if we leave just on daylight and get back just on dark, those public servant jerks won't be about.'

'What about the water police?' Bernie protested.

'They won't be about down here during the week,' Lincoln reasoned. 'It might be a bit more of a risk on the weekend. Anyway, if they come up to us at sea we've got no rego numbers. The cowls on the motors have been re-surfaced ready for the new decals so there's nothing to identify us. We'll just out-run 'em. Nothing to worry about mate, I guarantee.'

The cat's motors were large but their actual horsepower rating had been a bit of a mystery to Bernie when the boat first came into his yard. The cowls gave no clue but later, during routine service, it was apparent considerable rebuilding of the engines had taken place. The motors contained parts from both the 175 and 200 horsepower models. Bernie knew the motors were hotted up and in tip-top shape. He was confident no police boat would be able to out-run her. Despite this he did not feel as confident as Lincoln sounded.

'Perhaps it's just I'm not a seasoned crim like you,' Bernie protested. 'But the cops will just call in re-enforcements and they will get us eventually, won't they?'

'Look, trust me,' Lincoln reasoned. 'Over the years I've been the subject of a few high-speed chases with that Bayliss inspector bloke after me. A good boat chase is pretty exciting you know. That's action and that's why they put chases in the movies; to get the audience in.

That TV show, Water Rats, is tame compared to some of my chases. But the real world is not like the movies and in all my chases I've never ended up in court. They have to catch you red-handed with the contraband still on the boat. Besides, for them to be successful in a hot pursuit at sea, they might reckon they have the legal ability to demand a boat stop but that's only a minor consideration. Their real issue is their capacity to out-run us over time and distance. If you keep your face down and don't look at them they can't identify you so they can't win. I suppose if they had sufficient speed to lap us we could be in trouble, but they'll never lap us or out-run us this time. On the movies the goodies fire shots over the bow of the crook's boats and that seems to work but like I said, this ain't the movies. Are you in or out?'

'In, I suppose,' Bernie muttered. 'Sure could use a few extra bucks at the moment.'

'That's my man,' Lincoln smiled. 'Never say die, that's what I say. I've never surrendered in the past and I don't intend to start tomorrow. Meet you at the shed at five.'

Next day Greg and Kirby were on patrol in the departmental boat. This was also a Shark Cat the same size as the one from Bowtell's Boat Yard. The officers had no specific target but were anxious no craypots were in the water prior to the commencement of the season. Off Porpoise Head they discovered a couple of twenty litre drums floating and tied together with cable. When they investigated they discovered the drums had nothing to do with crayfish. They marked a line set for a shark. This sort of equipment would be legal but only if set and used by a licensed fisherman, and then it also had to be marked appropriately with the number of the fisherman's registered boat. As there were no markings on this particular gear they began to haul it aboard.

The line had caught an enormous manta ray that had died. The sheer weight of the creature, and two anchors made from metre-long pieces of railway line, gave the officer's a task of formidable proportions. The Shark Cat was nearly two and a half metres wide and the manta ray was visible to both Greg and Kirby as each looked over opposite sides into the water.

They finally managed to extract the hook, a wicked looking grapple apparently hand-forged by a blacksmith and nearly thirty centimetres long. The ray sank slowly into the gloom as they fought the tangle of cable, chain, hook and railway line over the gunwale and aboard. They left all this, together with the two drums, in a jumbled mess in the middle of the deck as they continued their patrol.

About four bays before they reached the lighthouse, a relatively low-lying white boat suddenly sprang up onto the plane in front of the officers and headed away at speed. Greg and Kirby jumped to the same conclusion together; it had to be poachers. Kirby, who was driving at the time, jammed both throttles forward as hard as he could and a spectacular boat race began.

The officers had a handicap of about a hundred and fifty metres. As they roared along, Kirby continually trimmed the motors and pushed again and again on the throttles. Pushing the throttles was futile in the circumstances but he was doing everything in his power to encourage all potential speed out of the patrol boat.

'What sort of a boat is it?' Kirby yelled to Greg above the tumultuous roar of their outboards.

'Dunno,' Greg answered. 'From the shape of the rooster tail water sprout behind, it looks like a Shark Cat but it's far too low in the water. I can't even see any people in her.'

As they neared the lighthouse Kirby had the impression they were gradually gaining. Visual contact was lost for a short time as the target disappeared around the headland. Greg signalled with his hands for Kirby to move closer in and to hug the coastline. This was to keep the distance as short as possible but Kirby did not know the territory. He did not feel comfortable doing it but he did not hesitate to follow the instructions given by his boss.

Once past the lighthouse the fleeing boat headed across the next bay and on towards Henty Heads. By the time Kirby reached Henty Heads there was no doubt the officers had little or no chance of apprehending their quarry.

'Give up?' Kirby asked.

'Never!'

'Who do you reckon it could be?' Kirby questioned.

'Dunno. Ab poachers.'

Kirby continued to adjust the trim of the motors and to push on the throttles. Nothing he tried made any appreciable difference. The boat in front now appeared to be getting smaller.

The sea had been relatively calm all the way but off Henty Heads, opposing tidal currents had created waves that rose sharply and steeply in an area of very turbulent water. Kirby had never seen waves that were so precipitous and close together. The path of the race went straight through this severely agitated sea.

'If they can do it, so can we,' Greg yelled as he indicated to keep her rolling.

Kirby was excited but knew they were wasting their time. He did as his boss encouraged. The deck of all Shark Cats is well above the water line and the transom between the motors cut away to form a scupper large enough to quickly clear vast amounts of water. The spray the boats created looked spectacular as they crashed through the waves at full steam ahead. In reality little water came aboard the patrol boat.

Rattle, bang, crash!

Kirby thought he had blown a motor. He looked around, expecting to see smoke billowing from one of the cowls. Instead he saw two twenty-litre drums trying to fit out through the scupper behind two pieces of railway line, a large hook and assorted cables and chain. The drums were never going to fit but the rest of the cargo already had! The image Kirby had of all that mess tangled around severely damaged outboard legs and wound tightly around two stainless steel propellers was not pleasant. Nor was the thought of the paperwork, and the intense relationship producing it, would mean for Kirby and FRED.

Kirby yanked the throttles back to neutral and switched off both motors. The officers then spent four or five valuable minutes recovering from their predicament. Eventually they managed to discard the whole kit and caboodle overboard. Kirby kicked the motors into life and gunned them to full throttle again. By now there was not even a small speck on the horizon. Kirby realized this meant FRED would not need to get involved and this lifted his spirits a little.

'Give up now?' It was more of a suggestion than a question. Kirby had felt the exhilaration of the chase, but despite this tried to be realistic about their likelihood of success.

'Not on your life,' Greg replied almost as if in a trance.

'But they're playing with us,' Kirby protested. 'I remember you telling me about Les Hoffmann speeding off and pretending not to know you were chasing him. This bloke is doing the same thing.'

Greg did not reply but motioned to keep going.

The boat had disappeared from sight but it appeared to be headed towards the mouth of the Paringa River. Kirby continued racing onwards and turned north into the channel marking the entrance. A few hundred metres in from the mouth a dredge was tied to a jetty but the target boat was nowhere to be seen. Before the river opened up into the inlet there were channel marks, professional fishing boats, private moorings and several jetties where a boat could hide. Kirby eased the throttles back.

Unexpectedly there she was again, travelling just as fast, out from behind the dredge and cutting across Kirby's bows from port to starboard. The boat was less than two hundred metres ahead! Kirby and Greg were about as close as when the contest began.

The chase was on in earnest again and the officers appeared to be keeping up as they raced generally northward in the inlet.

'Perhaps he hasn't ditched the bounty after all,' Kirby suggested after another minute.

'I don't know this area all that well,' Greg admitted out of the blue. 'Keep going, we're close.'

The water became shallow as they entered another small inlet. Both boats were soon following channels in the sea grass and these became very narrow.

'I don't like this much,' Kirby complained.

'It doesn't matter,' Greg encouraged. 'The other boat is a Shark Cat, the same size as this, and we're closing in for the kill. We're only fifty or so metres behind and if he can get up the channels so can we. I reckon he has no-where to go. This has to be a dead end.'

It was.

'We've got him!'

Kirby could see why Greg made the prediction. The two officers stood much higher in their boat than the suspects in theirs.

From the elevated position the end of the narrow, twisting channel was clearly visible. The water was about to give way to a very large expanse of exposed mud. Kirby slowed right down, to about twenty kilometres per hour for fear of a collision.

The first boat slowed down too, when the dead end was only fifty meters or so ahead. This was a little late and the boat skimmed across the mud with elegant ease. The mire eventually took its toll on both vessels. The first was about twenty metres into the mud from clear water and Kirby and Greg were about fifteen metres behind, only a few metres into the mud.

As captain Greg felt it was his duty to stay with the ship until the last possible moment.

'Quick,' he commanded. 'Get over there and see what they've got.'

Kirby abandoned ship into mud almost up to his crotch and Greg relayed their success by radio. They were too far from head office but he managed to reach Mellissa Elliot at the lighthouse.

'Can you stand by Mellissa?' Greg requested. 'We've just intercepted a boat load of suspected abalone poachers and may require some assistance. Over.'

Greg deliberately exaggerated the importance of the interception and had intentionally not been specific about what assistance may be required. He did not want to broadcast information about the patrol boat being aground on a sea of mud.

'Sure,' Mellissa came back. 'What's your location? Over.'

'North end of Paringa Inlet,' Greg responded. 'Can you tell me the time of high tide? Over.'

'Fifteen hundred at the lighthouse,' Mellissa replied. 'There are no abalone in Paringa Inlet. What's the story? Over.'

'It's a bit complicated,' Greg replied sheepishly. 'I'll tell you when I see you. Over.'

'Standing by.'

Meanwhile Kirby struggled across to the other boat, and while still standing in the mud, introduced himself to Lincoln Campbell and Bernie Bowtell.

'Good-day fellas,' he said without knowing who they were. 'My name is Kirby Wellington, Fisheries Inspector. Was there any reason for the great rush to charge up the end of this channel and run aground on the mud?'

'What's it to you? Ain't no law against it so you can piss off.' Lincoln's bad grammar and alarming aggression were confirmation he had been up to no good.

'One moment sir,' Kirby challenged back. He wished he had not been sarcastic in his introduction and instantly knew this was not going to be an easy task. 'As I said, I'm a fisheries inspector and it is my duty to inspect your boat. I'm coming aboard.'

'Not with that bloody mud all over you, you're not,' Lincoln exploded. 'You've got no valid reason for inspecting this boat. This here is Bernie Bowtell the boat builder and owner of Bowtell's Boat Yard. I'm working for him and we're doing sea trials. You can see the boat ain't finished. We need to test her speed and ballast ratios in differing conditions. That's got nothing to do with you or fishing. So, like I said, rack off, Noddy!'

'And who may you be, sir,' Kirby asked trying to keep some authority in his voice. He was pretty sure it didn't work. In a split second he realized this man may be Lincoln Campbell. He had visions of a bloodthirsty brawl in the pub, and if these thoughts were correct, Lincoln's medication was not working!

'I'm Lincoln Campbell, if it's anything to do with you.'

Kirby was dumbfounded. He turned to look at Greg as if hoping for inspiration. None came. All he could think of was Greg's instruction to him never to approach this person without advising head office of his intentions, without direct communications with the police and without the police being present. He had none of these and Greg was absolutely no help in the circumstances. He was fifteen metres away talking on the radio and quite unaware of a nasty predicament amplified by about sixty centimetres of sticky, stinking mud.

'Well if you are only involved in boat trials,' Kirby said slowly, trying to argue out loud as he weighed the options in his mind, 'why are you in a wet suit and why have you got a compressor and hookah hose in the boat?'

Kirby was standing at the rear of the boat as he spoke. He had a clear view between the motors, and with no transom as such, could see the entire deck area. There were no abalone unless they were hidden in one of the pontoons or in one of the small lockers under the dashboard. He doubted that.

'You're obviously as dumb as you are stupid looking standing there in mud up to your balls,' Lincoln grunted. He was obviously enjoying himself at the officer's expense. 'If something went wrong with one of the motors I could get in the water, and with a bit of luck, fix it. We're giving the motors a major re-build too.'

Kirby knew that explanation was just padding for an already very dubious story but he was ambushed. If he backed down, he compromised his authority but if he took the matter any further, he would disobey an instruction. Kirby turned and trudged back to Greg in the patrol boat.

'You didn't even get on the boat,' his boss scolded before he climbed back aboard the patrol boat. 'How could you have searched the boat properly?'

'I didn't. I couldn't,' Kirby answered. 'It's Lincoln Campbell and Bernie Bowtell, the boat builder. I reckon they were poaching all right. They've got a hooka unit but they wouldn't have had the abs when I got there. Even if it hadn't been for the instruction not to approach Lincoln without the police, I don't think I'd have been game to board that boat by myself. But just walking away, I can tell you I didn't like that much. He's playing us on a break.'

'Don't worry about it,' Greg comforted. 'You did the right thing believe me. Besides, if I know Lincoln Campbell, he'll have jettisoned his abalone in a way he will still be able to recover them. They'll be back tomorrow and we'll be ready for them. It's the opening of the cray season tomorrow and he will expect us to be working the cray fishery. We won't be and I wouldn't mind betting the abs are on the bottom near where we first saw the boat. That means they need a boat tomorrow to get them. They won't be able to swim out from shore during the night to get them. We'll just put our cray season work on hold. This is too good an opportunity to miss.'

'But he's over there laughing at me,' Kirby complained. 'Look at them.'

'Don't worry. You'll have the last laugh, I promise.' Greg was calm and reassuring. 'The last laugh is the best laugh and it will be worth it. Trust me.'

Using the headphones so Lincoln and Bernie did not hear, Greg was soon back on the radio to Mellissa. He made detailed arrangements about the next morning and asked her to contact the police. Half an hour later Mellissa called back and confirmed the plans. This included having an observer in place before daylight. They were to be on location overlooking the general area where Lincoln and Bernie had been when the chase began that day.

A few hours later high tide brought relief from the mosquitoes and the mud that had held the boats and men captive since early afternoon. Both boats re-floated about the same time. The officers made sure Lincoln could start his motors and they prepared to head for home. Lincoln called them over.

'I haven't got enough fuel to get home. Can you give me some?' he requested.

'Where is your boat trailer; where do you have to go?' Greg responded.

'You don't find out that easy,' Lincoln laughed.

'Well we can't give you fuel unless we know how much you need.'

Greg now had a slight psychological advantage. He laughed back at Lincoln.

Kirby's discomfort during the aborted boat inspection had changed to gross embarrassment. How could his boss play that sort of game with these buccaneers?

'I'll tell you what I'll do,' Greg called back. 'We'll follow you back to the mouth of the Paringa River. Once you're there at the jetty, you'll be OK. There is a public phone box near the shop and they sell outboard fuel.'

As they travelled down the channel, Lincoln kept an even distance behind. Once in the open inlet, Greg, who was now driving, gunned the patrol boat to three-quarter throttle. Lincoln easily kept pace. From there Greg gradually eased the speed up until the patrol boat was flat out again. Lincoln remained the same distance behind.

'Why do you play his stupid games?' Kirby asked. 'We know from before he can go as fast as we can. And I don't understand why we didn't just leave him when he asked for fuel. I would have pretended I didn't even hear him; that's what he did to us. He could rot in the mud for a month for all I care.'

'It's OK,' Greg consoled. 'I said before you would get the last laugh. Besides we don't want to be criticised for not rendering assistance to a boat in trouble. I doubt he needs fuel, but playing along like I have should see him drop his guard a bit for tomorrow. He'll be thinking he can play us on a break, especially if he thinks we're working the cray opening.'

Off the end of the jetty Greg did a turn to port and headed for the entrance. Lincoln turned to starboard and pulled into the jetty.

Next day at 10:30 Greg and Kirby met Jackie Blewitt at the police station. The three officers launched the patrol boat from the ramp at the northern end of Mafeking Bay. This ramp was used by anglers in the river and bay but not by boats travelling out to sea. One of the other police members drove the vehicle and boat trailer back to the police compound behind the station.

Sea conditions were just as ideal as the day before. They travelled at full throttle all the way. Even when they had crossed the comparatively dangerous waters of the entrance to the bay there had been no need to reduce speed.

Once out beyond Rocklyns Point Greg stopped and made radio contact with Mellissa Elliot and then the police station. Mellissa gave him the news he wanted. Greg immediately contacted head office with advice of his intention to intercept Lincoln Campbell. Greg, Kirby and Jackie headed straight back to where Lincoln had been the previous day. The trip took the best part of half an hour. As they neared the target area, Greg had taken over the radio as the official forward controller of the operation. Kirby was skipper and Jackie was observer. Greg made and answered numerous radio calls. The plan was working perfectly.

Lincoln and Bernie were in the same borrowed boat. The very low profile and white colour made it difficult to see at any distance, especially when it was stationary. Bernie saw the approaching patrol boat before the inspectors saw the poachers. On radio advice from Melissa, Greg was giving precise directions on the location of the pirates. Despite this, Kirby only saw their target when it jumped up on the plane and sped off. Greg had barked instructions to Kirby with military precision but the poaching pirates were under way within a few seconds of Kirby changing course to intercept.

Lincoln was unpredictable. Instead of taking off away from the patrol boat as expected, he headed straight back towards Mafeking Bay. This was virtually on a collision course with the patrol boat. Shark Cats at full speed are impossible to turn sharply. Even when Kirby had the motors on full lock the boat was quite safe but it leaned out of the corner, not into the corner like a conventional hull or a motorbike. Jackie, who had little boating experience, found this a little disconcerting as the centrifugal force tended to cause people on any catamaran making a turn, to also lean out. The forces made it difficult to keep balance.

Kirby had the wheel on full lock to starboard and the boat came around losing speed in the process. Lincoln was off like a startled rabbit and initially the distance between the two boats closed alarmingly. During the 180 degree boat turn Kirby came perilously close to the rocks and his heart jumped into a hard lump in his throat. Jackie and Greg watched, wide-eyed, but neither spoke.

A very large, very solid looking bommy, a large submerged rock, was lying quietly under the gentle waves. The route looked perilous. Had the sea conditions been anything but perfect, the bommy would have been quite obvious because of associated white water. Kirby shut his eyes as he expected disaster to contact either the bottom of the pontoon or the leg of a motor. Neither happened. The clearance had only been a centimetre or two.

By that time Kirby believed they had already missed Lincoln too, exactly as the day before. But Greg knew Mellissa had sufficient evidence in her observations and in the photos taken from shore through a telephoto lens.

Greg was busy on the radio relaying all the action back to the police station and head office. Switching between channels and twiddling knobs to try to improve the reception, Greg was on his knees with his head through the doorway into the radio compartment under the bulkhead. Kirby raced on after the speeding pirate.

With an additional person aboard the patrol boat, the distance between the two craft steadily increased as the distance between the boats and Mafeking Bay decreased. It was now blatantly obvious Kirby could not match Lincoln for speed. As the situation developed, Lincoln's reputation and unpredictability became very concerning but this did not give rise to any thought of aborting the chase.

'Do you want him?' Jackie inquired, unbuckling her revolver.

'Sure we do, but not dead,' Kirby said.

Jackie raised the weapon at arm's length, and holding it above the windscreen, took aim. It appeared to Kirby the target was the boat in front.

'You can't!'

Kirby was part way through his protest, when, boom! The firearm discharged. The officer was not a bad shot; she had not aimed anywhere near Lincoln, Bernie or their boat and consequently missed.

The noise was loud. Kirby was sure Lincoln heard it. All the previous day and so far that day, he had not even glanced behind. Immediately after the shot, Lincoln's head shot round and he half turned to look back at the pursing boat. This was a mistake on his part. Even if there was no immediate interception, the officers had seen his face and this would be useful for identification.

Kirby knew Greg heard it. Greg, unaware of the verbal exchange between Jackie and Kirby, was consequently startled by the revolver shot. The noise of the back of his head coming into contact with the bottom of the dashboard was clearly audible above the scream of the outboards!

'The radios' blown up. It's clagged!'

Greg was wailing and rubbing the back of his head. He was in obvious shock, just as much from the knock on the head as from what had happened. At first he simply did not believe what Jackie had done.

'You what?' he demanded. 'Lincoln will complain for sure. Then what?'

'Let me worry about that,' Jackie grinned. 'I doubt he will and if he does, I'll deny it. The serge won't press me on it. He knows you have to fight fire with fire and he knows Lincoln is the sort of bloke who only knows one sort of law. Come on, aren't you the radio operator with urgent messages to send? Get back down there and do your job.'

Lincoln did not stop. He travelled back into Mafeking Bay through a narrow channel, in the reef off Rocklyns Point. Kirby was about 400 metres behind at that stage and the thought of another encounter with a bommy was too much. Kirby went around the narrow channel losing additional ground.

As they headed up the channel a thick sea fog rolled in, even though it was not yet mid-afternoon. The bay was perfectly flat and Kirby followed the fleeing boat by its wake until they were well up into the lake. Here all trace of the fleeing pirates disappeared. Greg's radio messages to the local police on shore soon had confirmation that the Bowtell's Boat Yard four-wheel drive, with a Shark Cat trailer attached, was at the main boat ramp.

'We'll simply go there and wait,' Greg announced. 'Mellissa has observations of Lincoln diving and bringing bags back to the boat on two occasions. She has photos she says will even make Lincoln blush. He relieved himself full Monty and Mellissa says she couldn't help herself. There is so much detail in that photo Lincoln will not be able to argue the other photos don't have detail too. Detail of his abalone poaching with Bernie helping. She says there are no photos that exactly show abs but she is positive that there were abs and these have been left on the bottom out there. We'll get them. The abs as well as Lincoln and Bernie, I mean.'

'How can you be so sure?' Kirby demanded. 'We don't know where they are at the moment and without the crooks in actual possession of the abalone, we'll have our work cut out I bet. I don't doubt Mellissa saw what she says she saw but how will we convince the court of that?'

'I think you've been frightened by all the stories about Lincoln,' Greg explained. 'Each time the crooks work to a pattern, we can devise a plan to catch them. All poachers get harder and harder to catch the more experience we give them, but I like to think we get smarter too.'

'How are we going to find the abs?' Kirby asked, far from convinced. 'It'll be like looking for a needle in a haystack. Even if we get the abs, Lincoln will probably still convince the court someone else was responsible and he is an innocent bystander. He and Bernie were just out testing the boat when they spooked the real crooks who fled before the patrol boat came along. The abalone being in the same area doesn't prove a darn thing.'

'If Lincoln can find them, so can we,' Greg said quietly.

'Yeah, sure.' Kirby was dismal. His usual bright personality was being tested.

The young officer was still smarting from the humiliation Lincoln brought to bear the day before. He was now convinced Greg's promise of the last laugh was very hollow indeed.

'Besides,' Kirby continued. 'He knows where he left them.'

'So does Mellissa,' Greg calmly explained.

'Only the general area and their exact location won't be the subject of an admission, I bet.'

Kirby's continued protest seemed to be falling on deaf ears. He was getting sick of the argument.

'What do you reckon, Jackie?' Kirby asked turning to the police officer for support.

The radio crackled into life demanding Greg's attention. The police at the boat ramp reported the arrival of the fugitive boat and Jackie did not answer Kirby's question.

'We're on the way,' Greg responded. 'ETA ten minutes. Over and out.'

Lincoln and Bernie were standing on the ramp at the rear of their borrowed boat. It was now on its trailer and removed from the water behind the Bowtell Boat Yard four-wheel drive. A police divisional van effectively blocked the escape route. Lincoln was in a wet suit and a puddle of water had developed on the boat ramp where he stood. More water was draining from the bungs in the boat's transom as it rested on the trailer up the slope at the top of the ramp.

Mellissa and the shore-based crew drove up a couple of minutes after the patrol boat arrived. The police kept Lincoln and Bernie quiet as Greg and Kirby had a chat to Mellissa and her crew.

'We finally crept to within one hundred metres of the boat,' she explained. 'They had no idea we were there. The boat was only about fifty metres out from the rocks and through binoculars we made excellent observations. I already told you about the photos and Lincoln's twinkle over the side, didn't I? We were close enough to clearly see the radio aerial and net bags containing dark objects being taken aboard. You could see this without binoculars. I couldn't positively swear the bags contained abalone though. I suppose the defence will claim they were rocks or something.'

'No they won't,' Greg snapped. 'Well at least if they do, it won't solve their problems. Look, we all have to be positive about this. Negative thoughts always become self-fulfilling prophecies. What about a bit of positive thinking you lot? What did you say on the radio before about the bags being put back over the side Mellissa?'

'After the abalone, or whatever it was, were brought onto the boat they seemed to sort them or something into different bags. These bags looked like hessian bags to me. You know, like spud bags. Then they had these two dark grey things, about thirty centimetres long they each held over the side of the boat into the water. It looked like one of these things was put in the bag with the abalone and one was kept aboard. They were a bit different shape. One had yellow on it.'

'There,' chortled Greg. 'If we can find one of those things on the boat, we're home and hose.'

'What is it? Why is it so important to find one if there were two of them?' Mellissa asked.

'You find it and I'll show you,' Greg teased. 'No time for explanations now. Kirby and Mellissa, you search the boat. A real proper search mind you. Look for any possible false partitions. Check the batteries. They could be duds. Hollowed out, a big marine battery case can hold a couple hundred bucks worth of ab meat. Make notes of what you find, especially fish and fishing gear. Take photos of anything suspicious. Take a photo of any evidence with it still in situ if possible. Is there any recreational gear or is it all commercial poaching stuff? I'll get the police to try to hold these guys for another ten minutes or so. Look snappy now. Lincoln knows we can't hold them but we can search the boat and car. I'll do the car. If they start to leave, walk away I mean, we'll have to decide whether to arrest them or just let them go and give them a summons later.'

Lincoln knew exactly what was going on and decided attack was the best form of defence.

'Are we under arrest?' he bellowed. 'If not I demand you shift that bloody police car so we can go.'

'You are not under arrest,' Greg responded. 'You can go any time you like but you are not taking the boat or vehicle. We are going to search those and probably we will seize them. I have no doubt you two were engaged in a large scale abalone poaching operation yesterday and today.'

Greg would not normally tell a suspect about possible seizure until he had finished the search and questioning. Lincoln was different, and this situation was different in a number of ways. Greg knew Lincoln's challenge, that he intended to leave, was real. That meant there was no point in diplomacy. Lincoln could erupt at any moment, and as a result, the police would arrest him in order to keep the peace. At least then they could complete the searches without the hostility.

Kirby climbed up onto the boat. Sitting on its trailer it was much higher than when in the water or stuck on the mud. Once up on the deck Kirby turned to help Mellissa climb up. Greg approached the four-wheel drive. Lincoln stepped towards Greg and then changed his mind. He turned and ran towards Mellissa as Kirby hauled her up. Bernie stood flat-footed and mute.

'Bull shit. Get out of that boat!' Lincoln yelled. 'I told you the other day you've no bloody right here 'cos this is boat repair business. Not fishing. Git out! I'll bloody knock you heads off.'

The police were alert and Jackie and another officer grabbed Lincoln before he reached Mellissa. The moment Jackie touched Lincoln he spun around and began swinging wild haymakers. Jackie had moved in quickly and was closest to Lincoln. Once he decided to hit out at the police, it did not matter the first person he intended to flatten was a woman. Lincoln did not know much about karate or Jackie's black belt. He landed very heavily on his back with the wind knocked out of him. Before he realised it, Jackie had rolled him over on his stomach and handcuffed his wrists behind him. Gentle pressure on the back of his skull had him literally eating dust. Lincoln continued to resist but his oaths and profanities were now mild little grunts and his threats were harmless. Their volume steadily decreased.

Bernie still had not moved or made a sound. He thought he was on the set of the movie Waterworld with Kevin Costner where he played a pirate and there was lots of fighting on the water. With this thought he resolved to sack Lincoln and retire from abalone poaching immediately. Unfortunately for Bernie, he was implicated in the offences. He and Lincoln were to remain partners for some time yet.

Kirby and Mellissa found more than they, or Greg, had hope for. The boat still contained the hookah unit and hose. There were eleven hessian bags, a couple with Velcro strips around the top and draw strings in the bottom. These were wet and one had a stainless steel ring in the top and a parachute attached. There were no fishing rods or lines but there were a couple of tools with lanyards attached. These were typical of the devices used to remove abalone from the rocks and to then remove the meat from the shell underwater. The hessian bags were then used to hold and transport the abalone meat back to the boat.

The officers could find no secret compartments and the boat batteries were real. With the boat stripped down the way it was, the search was completed very quickly. In a compartment under the steering wheel Mellissa found an overnight bag and some food and drinks in a small eskie.

Kirby and Mellissa sorted through the overnight bag, removing its contents onto the middle of the deck. Apart from clean, dry clothes there was a diary and the dark grey and yellow device. These were all photographed in the bag as Greg had instructed.

The device carried the brand name "Neverlost" and inside the diary cover Mellissa found the warranty cards for a Neverlost Dive Unit and two Neverlost Boat Units. These were issued to Lincoln and had been purchased two weeks previously.

Kirby flicked through the pages of the diary. There were numerous names and telephone numbers that would make great intelligence.

'How did you go?' Greg asked when they jumped down from the boat.

'I think we found what you want,' Kirby answered, showing his boss the dark grey and yellow device. 'We found three warranty cards too but they are for two boat units and one dive unit. What does that mean? Are they using two boats?'

'I'll explain back at the police station. I think we best get these two back there and formally request their names and addresses. I'd love to leave them in the safety of the cells while we go and recover the abalone; but once we seize their boat, fishing gear and vehicle we can't hold them any longer. With no boat or gear we will have, in the eyes of the law, stopped them committing this offence or committing any others. I'm confident we have enough evidence to charge them now, but if we find the abs they're in real hot water.'

'What's this "if" bit?' Kirby teased. 'I thought you said "when." What about some positive thinking and all that?'

The police were only too happy to put Lincoln and Bernie in the divisional van for the ride to the station. Once they were safely inside the back of the van Greg yelled through the window that the boat, gear and vehicle were seized. The police soon left with the prisoners and Greg followed in the seized vehicle, towing the seized boat. Mellissa and Kirby were passengers. Mellissa's crew remained at the boat ramp with their vehicles and the patrol boat.

After the formalities at the watch house Greg officially interviewed Lincoln. During this process Mellissa put her observations but Lincoln made "no comment" responses to all the questions and observations. Kirby interviewed Bernie who had been worded up by Lincoln. Bernie did as he had been told and also made no comment.

After discussion with Greg and Jackie, the sergeant decided not to take any police action over the fracas at the boat ramp.

'You're both free to go,' Greg told Lincoln and Bernie. 'You will both receive a summons to attend court at a later date.'

'Your got nothing on us,' Lincoln hissed defiantly. 'I'll be making sure Bernie and Bowtell's Boat Yard sue you and the government for loss of income and wrongful seizure. That boat doesn't belong to me and it doesn't belong to Bernie. It's owned by a licensed pro diver. It's a registered fishing boat. I told you before you had no right to seize it. The owner'll have your guts for garters when he finds out what you've done. You've seized it from us doing sea trials after he left it at Bowtell's Boat Yard for repairs.'

'See you in court,' Greg responded with a smile. 'We're going back to get your abalone now. I'll post you the seizure receipt for the exact amount.'

'You'll rot in hell if you try to pin any abalone on me,' Lincoln hissed. 'Or Bernie either for that matter. We've done nothing wrong. Typical government bloody jerk. You only get your kicks from making someone else miserable, don't you? Well you bit off more than you can chew this time I can tell you.'

Greg, Kirby, Mellissa and Jackie walked out the back door of the station leaving Lincoln steaming at the counter with a new constable. Bernie was still silent.

'You were going to explain why there are two boat units and one dive unit,' Kirby prompted when they were all back at the patrol boat at the boat ramp.

'These Neverlost units emit electrical signals and are designed to give direction and range but they only work underwater,' Greg began to explain to a very attentive audience. 'That's why you saw Lincoln and Bernie holding them over the side earlier, Mellissa. They were testing them. Hanging one unit under the boat is the way most people use them. Multiple units can be programmed to work together, a bit like the remote sensors to open garage doors. People who have two or three cars can have a unit in each to open the one garage door. The divers take an underwater unit so the direction and range of the boat can be easily determined. It's easy to find your way back to the boat like that.

'Then some bright spark worked out these things were good for finding poached abalone left on the bottom. This was not smart really because the manufacturer advertises them for use by marine biologists finding their way back to survey sites and the like. The way the poachers use them is back to front. They leave the boat unit on the bottom, with the abalone, so they can find their way back to their bounty. They come back at night and mostly recover the abs from shore so we don't get the opportunity to seize the boat or gear. Anyway, I reckon the reason there are two boat units and one dive unit is because one boat unit is on yesterday's abs and one is on today's abs. If we can find both of them, we will find Lincoln's catch of abalone for two days.'

'Let's go,' Kirby prompted.

'Ok,' Greg agreed. 'Mellissa, we need you to go back to where you were so you can direct us into the area where you watched Lincoln and Bernie lean over the side. You need to go via the police station. I have arranged for two members to follow you out in a police car in case Lincoln comes out for a sticky-beak. Jackie, Kirby and I will be in the patrol boat again. See you there.'

Forty-five minutes later Greg leaned over the side of the patrol boat and switched on the underwater unit. There was an instant response and it took less than ten minutes to recover two hessian bags tied together and attached to an anchor with a buoy below the surface. The bags contained nearly five hundred abalone meats. This amount of abalone would fetch many thousand dollars on the black market.

Mellissa and Jackie were as happy as Kirby and Greg.

'Now for the big test,' Greg said. 'Let's see if we can find yesterday's fish. Kirby, you were driving when we first saw the boat. Where was it? I'll wager the abs are there and not in Paringa Inlet.'

'A couple of kilometres towards Rocklyns Point from the lighthouse I suppose,' Kirby responded. 'Heck, that's a bit of a tall order. All I remember is a low looking white boat suddenly appeared in front of us and we ended up miles from there, stuck on the mud in Paringa Inlet.'

'We were well past Porpoise Head,' Greg reasoned. 'That narrows it down to about twenty nautical miles. Let's give it a go. We won't know if we don't try and we've got a few hours before dark. I reckon I can put us within a couple of hundred meters. The distance out from shore shouldn't be too much trouble. They were in pretty darn close as I recall it.'

'What's the range of these things?' Kirby asked.

'Dunno,' Greg said honestly. 'Maybe seventy-five metres in good conditions. We'll find out with a bit of luck.'

They steamed off, looking for the spot.

'I remember,' Kirby suddenly announced. 'We were one or two bays this side of where you told me you first saw Les Hoffmann in his new purple ocean-racer. I remember seeing the lighthouse in front of us and after a pretty short while, I remember seeing the place where you said the purple boat was.'

'Good stuff. I reckon you're right. We'll start there because that's about where the reef starts again. For a mile or so this side of there it's a sandy bottom and surf beaches. It had to be after that.'

At the end of the surf beach, Kirby motored in to within about fifty meters of the shore and came to a stop. The plan was to stay the same distance off shore and motor along slowly, holding the Neverlost unit over the side. Provided the units were capable of a range of fifty metres or more, the officers expected they would be searching a band of water from the shore out at least one hundred meters. Kirby and Greg were sure the boat was closer in than when they first saw it.

Searching the length of the first bay proved fruitless, but just after the headland, the unit began to respond to a signal. Ten minutes later they had two more bags of abalone meat. These too were hessian bags and filled to capacity. They were tied together with the same cord and attached to an identical anchor with an identical buoy below the surface. Lincoln had had a good day. This time there were nine hundred and eighteen abalone meats.

'It's your shout,' Greg suggested to Kirby after reporting their success to Mellissa and the police station via radio. 'I said you would have the last laugh. What about we invite Mellissa and her crew and we have a few drinks at the pub to celebrate. Jackie, it'd be great if you and a few of your mates from the station could come too. What about it?'

Everyone agreed and after everything had been stowed for the trip, the patrol boat headed at speed for Mafeking Bay.

As expected, Lincoln contested the case when it eventually came up in court. At the conclusion of the case the prosecutor made application for cancellation of Lincoln's professional crayfish licence, forfeiture of the fishing gear, the borrowed Shark Cat and the Bowtell's Boat Yard vehicle. The boat owner and his lawyer were in court, and when given the opportunity they argued the monetary value of the boat far exceeded the seriousness of the crime, especially as the boat was not owned by either of the defendants. In addition, it was argued, the boat owner had no knowledge of the illegal use of his boat.

In summing up the court said it was prepared to cancel the defendant's crayfish licence on the basis he was not a fit and proper person to hold any type of commercial fishing licence. Over the years Lincoln had demonstrated an attitude towards the law the court could not ignore. Clearly this attitude meant the defendant could not be trusted with the privileges that flowed from making money from the publicly owned fish resources of Victoria. The court went on to say it understood this was a very significant punishment and it considered little else was required by way of penalty or deterrent to other people who fished.

The licence cancellation was gratifying news but the officers were bitterly disappointed when they failed to add another boat to Her Majesty's fleet. The forfeiture application was successful only in relation to the fishing equipment and car. The boat owner had travelled all the way to court from Melbourne and the magistrate made it clear he expected the boat to be returned to him, not to either of the defendants, as the legislation allowed. In addition the court was emphatic it be returned "today".

'We'll have to do something about this,' Kirby challenged Greg when they were outside the court. 'All the crooks will now register their poaching boats in a fictitious name and get one of their cronies to come to court and say they own it. We'll never get another boat forfeit to the crown.'

'Maybe there is something we can do,' Greg mused as he led Kirby back to the car. 'It's not usual for the crown to appeal a magistrate's decision, except on the basis of an error in law. The decision today to return the boat was not a question of law. The section clearly gives the court discretion to order it forfeit or authorise its return to the defendant or the owner. The magistrate may have been a bit over the top because he was emphatic it be returned today. In my mind that was an order and not simply an authorisation. The court power can only authorise its return but our salvation may be in the Director of Public Prosecutions. Without arguing the law, he can appeal if it is considered the penalty is manifestly inadequate in the public interest. I'll have a talk to Murray and see what he thinks. In the meantime you best return the boat. We don't want to upset the magistrate too much. If we get him off side, we might win this battle but the war with poaching in the long term is what we have to win.'

Kirby very reluctantly agreed. With his head spinning in circles and his mind off on all sorts of tangents Kirby began walking towards the departmental car. As he crossed the road to the car park. Lincoln's lady friend, Lorren Bibby, ran up and spoke to him. Well, Kirby imagined, by definition, it was speaking but it surprised him coming from a woman. In addition it surprised him it all happened in such a public place. Kirby had never heard the equal to that barrage of insults, threats and blasphemy. Afterwards though, he sort of appreciated her actions on the basis she was just minding her man. She knew, in effect, he no longer had a job. Kirby suspected she knew Lincoln would need to keep paying the bills and therefore be forced to engage in more unlicensed abalone poaching. In the weeks and months to come, Lincoln would continue to be mentioned in the department's black book on numerous occasions.

Chapter 6

Kirby eventually extracted himself from Lincoln's lady friend. After he had written out a receipt for the return of the boat, he returned it to the owner who promptly took it back to Bowtell's Boat Yard for storage.

First thing next morning, Greg and Murray began the process of putting the possibility of an appeal up through the channels. This involved an immense amount of internal politics and meant a lot of urgent paperwork for Kirby, FRED and Greg.

A couple of days before the deadline for lodging the appeal, the Director of Public Prosecutions agreed. It was in the public interest, to protect abalone stocks and the industry from poaching, that boats used in large scale illegal operations should be forfeited to the crown. On this basis an appeal was lodged against the magistrates' court decision.

As part of the affidavit material, the Crown argued the owner of the boat, a licensed abalone diver, should not be aggrieved by this course of action. If the judge did eventually forfeit the boat, this would set precedence in other matters where borrowed equipment was seized from poachers.

The affidavit argument was to the effect that the only proper course of action, for the long-term protection of the industry, was forfeiture. After all, this industry was the boat owner's own industry. Surely he would want it protected. The purposes of the Act supported this submission because it talked about "the welfare of the fishing industry and those engaged in it."

Besides, the boat owner had a clear legal remedy against the boat yard; civil proceedings for damages.

The local paper ran the story but the public did not care. During the period when the officers were waiting for the appeal to be listed the saga developed in a couple of directions.

Kirby often drove past Bernie's Boat Yard keeping tabs on the Shark Cat. Bernie had finished the repairs, sprayed on a new coat of gel-coat and replaced all the decals on the motors. It looked like a different boat, almost brand new except for some modifications to the inside lower portions of both pontoons.

The second thing that happened related to Lincoln's lady friend. She was more than just a tad upset at the cancellation of the crayfish licence. In her mind, and no doubt in Lincoln's too, it was unfair to cancel a crayfish licence when the offending related to abalone.

Beginning with the altercation outside court, and for a period of several months, Lincoln's lady friend made numerous calls to Kirby and to the department's licensing section. Kirby soon lost all benevolent feelings towards a lady just "minding her man."

She invariably spoke to one of the junior clerks and subsequently, when Kirby discussed his phone calls with a colleague in the licensing section, he discovered none of the calls contained best wishes or good luck.

Everyone who took the calls took the brunt of abuse and obscene language. Invariably this became acutely personal and vitriolic. Kirby always made notes of the calls he received and asked the staff in licensing to do the same. Dates, times and content of the calls were recorded.

Kirby had no qualifications to make the judgement but he considered this lady needed help and needed it now, before he needed a doctor or undertaker. The voice of the caller was very distinctive and she did not try to hide her identity. At the beginning of the conversations Kirby's demeanour was frequently calm and logical, but the subject was always the same. Lincoln's plight was Kirby's fault and she was going to ensure that actual responsibility fell on Kirby. What that looked like was always spelled out in detail.

Kirby knew already that in a household with one income, all members suffered when the income stopped. Lincoln was penniless and the barrage of insults, threats and blasphemy Kirby received outside court began to degenerate even more. In the weeks that followed the threats to kill and threats to inflict serious injury became very real and more violent. Kirby's anxiety increased. He had no doubt if ever the two came face-to-face, Lorren would attempt to put at least one of her promises into effect. Kirby was too young to die and some of her suggested methods were indeed grotesque. Kirby had no doubt Lincoln's past life and pub brawls had rubbed off on his girlfriend. He also expected Lincoln would know of the intervention on his behalf, if he wasn't actually the driving force behind it.

Kirby rang Telecom Investigations.

'Yes,' they said, 'this type of call is against the Commonwealth Telecommunications Act.'

Kirby gave them the name of the caller.

'Can you tell me where she is ringing from?' they wanted to know.

'No, I'm sorry I don't know that. I think she rings from a public phone box.' This was based on his belief Lincoln had recently had his telephone disconnected. He gave them Lincoln's address.

'Well, if you can't tell us where the calls are made from, and you are not able to tell us exactly when she will ring you next, I don't think there is much we can do. Don't hesitate to ring back if I can be of additional assistance to you.'

Kirby was hardly grateful for the co-operation and told the investigator so as he slammed down the receiver. He was shaking just as acutely as he did after each of the abusive and threatening phone calls.

When the frequency and intensity of the calls increased even more Kirby spoke to his doctor about the consequences on his health. He eventually also spoke to Greg and discussed what he suspected was a pretty serious health problem.

Greg knew of the calls and eventually worked out Kirby was not handling the pressure at all well. Kirby took Greg's advice and spoke to Jackie Blewitt at the police station. She was sympathetic and reassuring. As she took a statement, she was positive something could be done.

'Leave it with me. I've got a few contacts and I'll make a couple of enquires. We'll do something about this.'

That is exactly what happened. The police arrested and charged Lorren Bibby under the Victorian Crimes Act. She faced a large number of charges of threat to kill. There were an equal number of charges of threatening to cause serious injury. The dates of these charges were based on the notes Kirby had made during and immediately after the phone calls.

Unbeknown to Kirby, Jackie Blewitt or the local police, the police prosecutions section made contact with the Commonwealth Director of Prosecutions and a political tug of war began. The commonwealth wanted a piece of the action and argued there should be additional charges related to using a carriage service (telephone) to menace, harass or offend. With this political wrangling taking place, the matter was repeatedly adjourned and did not come on in court for over a year. After her arrest Lorren stopped ringing anyone on Lincoln's behalf; a relief for all.

Chapter 7

A day of so before the hearing of the appeal about the Shark Cat, Kirby photographed the boat on its trailer in the driveway of Bowtell's Boat Yard.

'Look at this photo,' he said to Greg when he got back to the office after picking up the prints. 'Why do you reckon the boat is parked in the driveway?'

'They're probably going to get rid of it before the court case,' Greg joked. 'I don't know. The owner is probably coming down from Melbourne to do a spot of fishing.'

On the morning of the court the Shark Cat was gone. At court the honourable judge agreed the decision of the magistrate to return the boat was not in the interests of the public, especially considering the value of the abalone industry. He ordered forfeiture to Her Majesty. This order was made despite the length of the arguments put forward by the respondent's barrister. His point was the court could not make such a forfeiture order because the boat had been disposed of and its whereabouts were unknown!

This cut no mustard with the learned judge. He read from the act, pointing out the forfeiture power of the court. This power, he said, was subservient to only two things. Firstly, there had to be a conviction and secondly, the seizure of the boat had to have taken place prior to the court making its decision. Ownership was irrelevant and the legal prerequisites to the court's forfeiture power were clearly met in this case.

Her Majesty at last had legal ownership of the boat but Kirby still felt he had been cheated out of his last laugh. Lawful ownership was one thing but physical possession was a different story.

The fact Lincoln had another conviction and forfeiture order against him did not deter his abalone poaching. With each conviction Lincoln was fined more and more, but the more he was fined the more he needed money. The more money he needed the more frequently he went abalone poaching.

Greg and Kirby knew Lincoln was heavily into illegal abalone but were mystified as to how he was doing it. The scheme Lincoln and Bernie worked out used a great variety of boats and the two pirates did not use the same boat regularly. In this way there were no public reports of this or that boat acting suspiciously. Lincoln made sure no pattern developed in his poaching so the officers could not work out his modus operandi and devise a plan to catch him.

Bernie had vowed never to go out in a boat with Lincoln again but their relationship had not ended as Bernie had hoped. Lincoln made the boat yard proprietor an offer he could not refuse.

'Look,' Lincoln offered. 'I'll pay your fines for you and I'll pay the business back to compensate for the forfeiture of the car. All I need is the full time use of the back part of the shed and for you to keep quiet about what's going on.'

Bernie simply did not have the strength of character to say no.

Lincoln began to build fibreglass boats in the back part of the shed at Bowtell's Boat Yard. This was partitioned off to prevent visitors getting even the slightest glimpse of what was going on. Lincoln combined his considerable experience operating boats with the skills he gained while working at the boat yard, and very quickly, became a competent boat builder. He breached copyright and made two moulds by using second-hand boats taken to the yard for repairs.

Lincoln personally tested every boat before they were sold through Bowtell's Boat Yard. In this way Lincoln always seemed to have a different boat to go poaching in, and Bernie seemed to be involved in a successful, legitimate business.

Lincoln was never afraid of hard work and whether he was at the yard or at sea, he was always at work before daylight. He always hid his car in the shed when at the yard and never left his car at the boat ramp when he was at sea. In addition he used a variety of boat ramps on his poaching trips. Eventually Kirby realised that an intimate relationship continued to exist between Lincoln and Bowtell's Boat Yard.

In the meantime the officers at Mafeking Bay waited for developments in relation to an Australian-wide bulletin sent to all fisheries and police departments. This sought assistance finding the missing Shark Cat. The photos taken by Kirby in the driveway of Bowtell's Boat Yard were posted on notice boards in virtually every coastal police station and fisheries office throughout the country.

Eventually it worked. South Australia reported a suspicion one of their licensed abalone divers, Adam Harvey, had the royal boat. The department obtained considerable legal advice and a letter of introduction from Victoria's Chief Commissioner of Police to his South Australian counterpart. Thus armed Kirby, Greg and Murray Stephens set off for Pomona on the York Peninsula, South Australia.

They took two vehicles, a hired Holden sedan and the Mafeking Bay four-wheel drive towing a suitable Shark Cat trailer. The entourage presented themselves to Police Headquarters in Adelaide, and although they did not get to meet the top bureaucrat, the Assistant Commissioner was most helpful. He rang the South Australian Criminal Investigation Branch at Kadina and made the appropriate arrangements for the Victorian posse to meet the local police there.

Next day the officers travelled to Kadina to rendezvous with the police as arranged. From there they travelled in convoy to Pomona, a short drive by car. At Pomona they discovered Adam Harvey was away fishing at Brenhouse Bay and staying in a caravan on the southern end of the peninsula. The police were familiar with the caravan park there and arrangements were made for a dawn raid the following morning.

The plan to strike while the diver was still in bed involved the three Victorian Fisheries Inspectors and three South Australian Police Officers. Just as the sun broke through the clouds on the horizon they entered the caravan park and examined the boat.

'It's the same one all right,' Kirby whispered excitedly. 'Look at the inside bottoms of the pontoons. They're unique. Look at the photo I took the day before it disappeared from Bowtell's Boat Yard.'

Kirby passed the photo round as proof.

'Look! It's absolutely amazing! This is the same tailer as in the photo.'

To Kirby's surprise the trailer carried no South Australian registration; just the expired Victorian one. The dilapidated number plate was now too rusty to be easily seen but the raised outline of the digits was still distinguishable.

Adam Harvey was half asleep and far less than half dressed when he answered the police knocks on his caravan door. When the question of boat ownership sank in the South Australian diver reeled back in disbelief. He realised he was not going fishing that day and his protest was desperate.

'My abalone entitlement is on that boat,' he protested. 'Before I will be allowed to go fishing again it will have be transferred to a new boat. I don't have another boat and the bureaucrats in Adelaide will take forever to manage it!'

Kirby, Greg and Murray had travelled a long way to get Her Majesty's boat and they didn't waste too much time worrying about

Adam's administrative problems. Murray served a certified copy of the court order of forfeiture. Kirby and Greg removed all the gear not covered by the order. When that task was completed Adam continued to co-operate. The diver used his tractor to back the boat and trailer into the water. Kirby then drove the forfeited boat off its trailer and ran it up onto the Victorian one. That night the posse reached Adelaide headed for home towing the bounty.

Kirby had friends who lived in suburban Adelaide and the officers intended hiding the seized boat up their driveway that night. When Kirby turned into the narrow street where his friend lived, there was an F100 utility double-parked and blocking the carriageway. The driver chatted to two men on the nature strip opposite. Kirby stopped and waited a few doors along from his friend's house. Instead of the offending driver shifting to allow Kirby through, he alighted from his vehicle and the three people approached.

'What are you doing with Adam Harvey's boat?' one demanded. 'He's a mate and I thought he was down at Brenhouse Bay fishing this week.'

Murray and Greg, who had been following in the hire car, arrived just in time. After some very fast talking, the two men reluctantly moved away and the driver of the F100 moved it to let Kirby through. He dared not glance sideways as he drove past his friend's house. Murray rang the police contact from headquarters and made arrangements to hide the boat for the night in a police compound not far from Adelaide Airport. From a motel Kirby rang and squared off with his friend as to why they weren't leaving the boat in his driveway.

The officers arrived safely in Melbourne and left the boat in a secure departmental store. Just as Kirby and Greg arrived back in Mafeking Bay they received a radio call from head office.

'Is Greg still with you?' Murray asked when Kirby answered.

'Sure is,' Kirby responded cheerfully. 'He's listening.'

Murray could tell from Kirby's voice the young officer was still enjoying his last laugh. The recovery of the boat from South Australia was a great climax to Kirby's first run in with Lincoln Campbell.

'I've got some bad news,' Murray said. 'That bloody Adam Harvey has issued a Supreme Court Writ against the State of Victoria and us three personally. The writ claims unspecified damages and loss of income resulting from his inability to continue his lawful occupation as a licensed abalone diver. I don't have to tell you two, ab divers make squillions and these proceedings could become mega expensive if we don't win. I hate to think what the damages could be. It will take years for the Supreme Court to list this matter and we'll just have to wait it out.'

A shudder ran up Kirby's spine as he recognised this probably meant his last laugh was a long way off, if he was ever to have it.

Chapter 8

During all this saga Kirby had kept plodding along doing part time study for the degree he was undertaking. It was hard finding time to do anything properly and occasionally he had to attend the campus in Melbourne for a day or two as part of the assessment for one or other of his subjects. Kirby had recently been informed, for the assessment on another subject; he had to prosecute a contested court case. It was a factual departmental file and was to be heard and determined at the Magistrates' Court at Costerfield.

The venue for the case had been shifted to Costerfield as it suited both the prosecution and the defence in this instance. All these arrangements were in place when Kirby received the official file several weeks prior to the court date.

With everything else that was happening at work, Kirby had not done much more than read through the file. The main witness was a fisheries inspector with considerable experience. He had a good number of successful court cases to his credit and Kirby considered all was well.

At court on the morning of the hearing, his preparations were not a lot better but he had prosecuted a few cases before, and he reasoned, knew what to do. In addition he expected the department would not have given him a file that was too difficult, even though there would be pleas of "not guilty." In truth the case was chosen and allocated to Kirby solely on the basis of a date that suited the assessor.

At court he announced his appearance, spoke to the defence lawyer and spent some time with the two departmental witnesses. They were confident everything was okay and they were ready to proceed.

Kirby knew sitting around waiting for a case to be called could be very boring. Despite this he was sitting in court when it opened at ten o'clock. He had been taught this was a courtesy, a show of respect that also demonstrated the prosecutor's readiness to proceed.

It was also a good practice because it presented an opportunity to adopt any good practices he could pick up from the legal profession. He knew it would also be a chance to learn how to avoid mannerisms and pitfalls of those who were not so proficient. He intended to watch the court room etiquette, scrutinise cross examination techniques, and most importantly, get to know the magistrate. He knew some had personal phobias and pedantic ways, and if he had not seen this magistrate before, he might learn some important indicators to help him with his case. All this was noted by the assessor.

On this occasion the Magistrate was Mr J. R. Austin, a very patient gentleman. A case was called that involved a relatively young offender charged by the police with stealing a bike. The defendant had pleaded guilty and was unrepresented. At the end of the policeman's evidence, the magistrate asked:

'Do you have any questions you wish to ask the policeman?'

'No. What he said is right.'

The police prosecutor closed the case and Kirby had the distinct impression this young man would probably get a good behaviour bond. If he was articulate enough to express his remorse to both to the court and the police, and clever enough to also say he had learnt his lesson, there was no reason why he should have a conviction recorded against his name.

'Is there anything known?' asked the magistrate. This was usual court room jargon that really meant, "Has this person ever been convicted of an offence before? Don't tell me about any cases which were dismissed, but if he has been put on a good behaviour bond or been given an official warning, then now is the time to tell me. I am about to impose a penalty in this matter, and if this person has committed similar offences in the past, this will be reflected in the penalty the court imposes today."

'Yes, your worship. Stand up please defendant.'

The prosecutor shuffled the papers on his file and read out a long list of prior convictions. There was nothing too serious, but the accumulation of so many brushes with the police clearly demonstrated a lack of regard for the law. No magistrate could take such a list lightly. Kirby changed his mind; this fellow was in trouble.

'Well, what do you want to tell me about all this?' the magistrate asked the defendant. His voice was most tolerant considering the length of the prior conviction history.

'Nothing your honour.' That was one of the things Kirby did know already. In those days people who called magistrates "your honour", demonstrate some knowledge of the county court where serious indictable offences are heard and determined. Not a clever thing to say when before a magistrate. (Magistrates are called "your honour" today).

'Of course you don't have to say anything, but is there someone else here to give evidence for you?' The magistrate's words were kind and encouraging.

'Me mum is here.'

'Your mother? You want her to give evidence for you, do you?' enquired His Worship.

'Is that all right?'

The clerk called the defendant's mother and she walked forward and entered the witness box.

'Now, what can you tell me about your son?' At this encouragement from the magistrate the character evidence began.

'When he was little, he was a lovely baby. I think it was when he fell out of his pram and landed on the cement that he changed. He's terrible now, has been ever since really. At school he was always in trouble and I can't make him do anything. He steals the money from my purse without asking and . . .'

'Wait a minute,' the magistrate interrupted. 'I've heard enough bad things about your son. The police have told me what he did that caused him to be in court today, and they have told me about his prior convictions. I want you to tell me something good about him.'

'Oh, I can't think of anything good,' his mother said thoughtfully.

'There must be something,' the magistrate encouraged. 'Does he have a hobby?'

The witness paused. 'He likes bikes.'

'Good,' said the magistrate.' He has a bike does he?'

'Yes. Err, well, he used to have one.'

'And what happened to it?' The magistrate was most patient and still encouraging.

'Well he took it apart and buried it.'

There was no emotion in the response. It was as if this sort of thing was normal, but the entire court erupted in an outburst that showed no respect for the dignity of the occasion, the court or the sad plight of the mother and her child. Kirby's case was called during the eruption of laughter that followed.

The defendant was an amateur fisherman charged with taking in excess of the bag limit for squid. He had several prior convictions for the same thing and this current case involved obstruction of the detecting officer. Kirby had to forget the extraordinary case he had just witnessed and present his case in a totally professional manner. Murray Stevens and a university assessor were in court.

Kirby's defendant had been under suspicion for some time. Reliable reports indicated the person was unemployed and fished for squid on five or six days a week, weather permitting. The officer's observations corroborated this. There was no doubt in his mind, this person was a "shameteur," a shameful amateur fisherman who illegally sold his catch.

The statement on file explained how the officer had observed the defendant and one other person, fishing for squid. The two people were in a boat in the southern section of Port Phillip Bay. The officer, making observations from the shore, counted twenty-three squid caught by the occupants of the boat. With this species having a bag limit of ten per person per day, the officer decided his best course of action was to make the interception while the boat was still at sea. Previous inspections revealed nothing when the defendant retrieved his boat from the water. There was good reason to suspect some clever shenanigans to land the excess catch without detection.

A radio call soon saw a second officer arrive, departmental boat in tow. The two officers confidently motored out to intercept. When they came alongside, and asked to see his catch, the defendant chucked a giant wobbly. He refused to facilitate this and instead steamed off. He subsequently began to throw squid overboard. Some floated in a plastic bag but the officers in hot pursuit of the fleeing pirate had not stopped to collect the evidence.

The fisherman eventually stopped his boat it allowed the principal departmental officer to board and conduct an inspection. There was not one squid on the boat.

The evidence of the first officer followed the statement on the file closely enough. When the cross-examination began, the officer assured the court he had seen, and counted twenty-three individual squid when he made his observations from shore. The defendant was already fishing when first seen and he was still fishing when the officers first arrived in the boat. This suggested there had been considerably more than twenty-three squid involved.

Up to this point, Kirby was confident his assessment would be going okay. The direction of the cross-examination then took three unexpected turns.

The first of these related to a bucket.

'When you were watching my client from the shore, you would have seen him lean over the side of the boat with a bucket, wouldn't you?' questioned the lawyer.

'Yes, I think I remember that,' said the officer.

'In fact he did this on a large number of occasions, did he not?'

'Yes, he may have.'

'You did not tell the court of this observation during your evidence in chief did you?'

'No.'

'Can I take it then you did not even record these incidents in your statement?'

'It is not in my statement.'

'Is it in your notes? I presume you did take notes did you?'

This was two questions in one and the opportunity Kirby had been waiting for. To show the assessment team his prowess as a prosecutor, Kirby jumped to his feet with an objection. The court upheld the objection and compelled the lawyer to ask the two questions separately. This little win was the only joy Kirby had for the rest of the case.

Having obtained admissions there was no mention of a bucket in his notes or statement, the lawyer went for the king hit; but only on the first point. At that time Kirby did not realise there was more to come.

'I put it to you this omission regarding the bucket is a deliberate attempt on your part to try to deceive the court. What do you say to that?'

The lawyer appeared smug as he waited for the answer. He did not have to wait long.

'That is absurd! It was not relevant,' came the indignant reply from the witness box. 'The buckets were just used to get water to the boat because squid, when they are caught, squirt black ink and it makes a mess in the boat. The water in the buckets was to wash down the boat.'

'If in your opinion it was not relevant, you would not have taken a lot of notice of my client at the particular time, that is, when he was leaning over the side, would you?' continued the lawyer.

'Not specifically, no,' said the officer.

'My client will give evidence, supported by his friend, the activity with the bucket did involve getting water as you suggest. However he will say the water was not for the purpose you assumed. The water in the bucket actually facilitated the return of excess squid to the sea unharmed. If you did not take specific notice of the activity with the bucket, you will not be able to deny it, will you?'

The court had every right to give little weight to the spluttered answer to this question.

'It is true, is it not,' continued the lawyer, 'squid do not have scales but rather a delicate skin which is damaged at the touch of the human hand?'

'Yes.' The reply was very sober indeed.

'The correct way to return a squid to the water unharmed is to refrain from touching it with one's hands, is it not?'

'Yes.'

'And squid jigs have hooks with no barbs and it is not necessary to touch the squid to get it off the hook is it?'

'That is correct.'

Enough points scored on the bucket. The lawyer moved to his next point.

'Now, in your evidence in chief, you said you knew the defendant and the defendant knew you and that you are a fisheries inspector. Is that correct?'

'Yes, that is correct.'

'In fact the first words you spoke when you came alongside were, "Good day Sisto. I'd like to look at your squid." This was your evidence in chief. Do you still say it is correct?'

'Yes.'

'You did not tell him you were a fisheries inspector, did you?'

'I did not have to. He knows me.'

'That does not answer my question. In case you are having difficulty, let me repeat it for you. You did not tell him you were a fisheries inspector, did you?'

'No.'

'And your partner did not tell my client he was a fisheries inspector, did he?'

'No, he was driving the boat. I don't think he spoke to the defendant at all.'

'Now this boat you were using. It was about four metres long, an open boat and not in any way marked except for the registration number. Is that so?'

'That is correct.'

'The purpose of using an unmarked boat is so you can approach suspect boats without them realising your identity. Is that the case?'

'Yes.'

'And on this day you achieved your aim. You motored right alongside my client before there was any communication from either boat to the other. This is true, isn't it?'

'Yes.'

'Now my client will give evidence, again supported by his friend, your approach coincided exactly with their intention to leave. The facts of the matter are my client already had the motor started and his friend had not stowed some of the gear correctly as he had been asked. He had continued to fish and the altercation on the boat when you approached was my client yelling at his friend. This yelling had two motives. Firstly, it related to some squid that had gone off in a plastic bag left in the sun. Secondly, the boat had not been readied for travel as my client and his friend previously agreed. He motored off with no consideration of you or who you were. You cannot deny that, can you?'

'That is not how I perceived the situation.'

Again the officer had not answer the question. This was getting him into hot water, and the water was getting hotter and deeper. The lawyer moved on.

'In your evidence in chief, I understood you to say your first demand for him to stop did not occur until after he was under way. Is that correct?'

'Yes, about that time.'

'It is true, isn't it, that squid fishing takes place with the boat drifting? It is common for the motor to be frequently started to move back over a productive area?'

This was two questions in one again but Kirby decided not to object as this issue was not in dispute.

The lawyer continued. 'Now when you made your demand to stop, you have no evidence my client knew you were acting officially, do you?'

'He knows who I am.'

'That does not answer the question and it's what you say to try to cover up the deficiency in your evidence. The fact remains, you have no evidence my client even recognised you, let alone recognised you as someone in authority, have you?'

The lawyer's comment about deficiency in the evidence was as objectionable as it was true. The officer eventually stammered out some kind of painful admission to the obvious delight of the lawyer.

'When you made your demand to stop, you have no evidence my client even heard you above the noise of his boat motor and your boat motor, do you?'

'Not directly but he knows who I am. He looked at me from only a couple of metres.'

The officer was attempting to plug the hole everyone in the court room was able to see. His repeated assertion the defendant knew him was tending to suggest this person had been in trouble with the law in the past. Kirby was beginning to worry about this. Such a disclosure could result in the court having to disqualify itself on the basis of bias against the defendant. Kirby need not have worried. The defence had a motive in letting the court know the defendant had prior convictions in relation to taking excess squid. This motive led to the next attack in cross-examination. It proved to be fatal.

'Yes,' continued the lawyer. 'You and my client are well known to each other because you have booked him in the past for taking excess squid, haven't you?'

The suggestion was true but it was not usual for the defence to actually want the court to know about prior convictions at this stage of proceedings. It is customary for courts to make decisions on the facts surrounding the case in question; without the distraction of past brushes with the law. Disclosure of this during the trial may prejudice the final decision. In this case Kirby now recognised the defence had something else up their sleeve.

'You know my client is a very keen squid fisherman, don't you?'

'Yes. He fishes for squid on five or six days a week, weather permitting.'

This was the witness attempting to get in a punch below the belt, or do the prosecutor's cross-examination job, or both. Kirby suspected the magistrate saw the foul and the end was in sight.

'Yes, that's right. There is no law against it, is there?'

'No.'

'And on this day you actually saw my client catching squid and you expected him to have well in excess of the bag limit on his boat. You say you saw twenty-three caught. Is that correct?'

'Yes'

'That is above the combined bag limit for the two men on the boat?'

'Yes.'

'Now, in the circumstances, it was natural for you to expect those excess squid to still be on the boat. You know my client is a very keen squid fisherman; he has even got prior convictions for taking in excess of the bag limit. You admit you took no specific notice of what my client did with the bucket when he repeatedly reached over the side of the boat. When my client left the fishing grounds you had pre-conceived ideas about what was on his boat, didn't you?'

'I knew there had been at least twenty-three squid taken onto that boat. I believed they would have caught some before I arrived and more after I left shore to go out in the boat.'

'Thank you. That is exactly my point. You knew what you were going to see before you saw anything didn't you?'

'What do you mean?'

'What I am putting to you is you were biased against my client. You did not investigate this matter. You thought you knew what was going on and you let your imagination prevent the collection of the evidence. You did not count the squid that were floating in the plastic bag, did you?'

'No.'

'You did not examine the bag to determine what else, apart from squid, was in it did you?'

'No.'

'You did not examine any squid that were in the bag to determine if they were fresh, did you?'

'No.'

'This bag was large and made of thick, opaque plastic which distorted your ability to see the contents, wasn't it?'

'Yes.'

Eventually the cross-examination concluded. Kirby's re-examination did nothing to repair the damage. The second prosecution witness added little, if anything of substance. He said he had not seen any squid caught and could not tell how many were in the bag he had seen discarded from the defendant's boat. His evidence about introductions, or the lack of an official identification during the introductions, did nothing to harm the defence.

The lawyer's no case to answer submission was predictable. He succinctly explained the evidence of the prosecution was unreliable in relation to key points on both charges.

Firstly, the prosecution had not discharged its burden, beyond reasonable doubt, as to the number of squid on the defendant's boat at any time or when the defendant left the fishing ground.

Secondly the defence should not have to answer the obstruction charge for two reasons. Initially the prosecution had failed to prove the defendant recognised the officer as a person he knew, let alone a person in authority. In addition to this fatal flaw the prosecution had failed to prove the defendant heard the demand to stop. The defendant did stop after some time; when he realised who the person in the second boat was.

Nobody was surprised when the court dismissed all charges and awarded costs in the defendant's favour.

After collecting his papers from the bar table, Kirby spoke to the witnesses. They were magnanimous in accepting the case was not lost for want of a decent prosecutor. Despite this reprieve, Kirby was dreading the prospect of an unfavourable appraisal. He approached Murray and the assessor who were sitting, talking in the court foyer. Kirby stood out of earshot until Murray indicated they were ready for him.

'How do you think you went?' he asked.

'I was ambushed. The statements on the file didn't contain the truth, the whole truth and nothing but the truth.' Kirby was not going to take all the responsibility for the case being dismissed. He was sure the assessment would be a disaster, like the case itself.

'Our assessment criteria relates to the prosecutor, not the witnesses. So how do you reckon you went?' The assessor now asked.

'I nearly had a fit when our matter was called just after the debacle with the kid who buried his bike. Hopefully I recovered okay from that but I'm not too proud of the result, I can tell you. In fact I feel really dreadful. It's enough to make me want to quit.'

'No you won't!' Murray was horrified at the thought of Kirby quitting. In an attempt to appease the disillusioned officer he continued.

'Like I said, this assessment is about the prosecutor, not the witness. Your recent annual career evaluation shows you're set for a bright future in this job. Not like a couple of other officers we could talk about. We're stuck with a few no-hopers who won't leave because they couldn't get another decent job if they left. You know about officers being forced back to head office because of incompetence, or sometimes worse. I don't have to name them I'm sure.

'Your general work and your performance as a prosecutor today are not at fault. A little bird just told me you scored an "A." There was nothing any prosecutor could have done to change the outcome given the way the evidence unfolded. Congratulations.

Kirby sort of thought he felt better.

Chapter 9

By the next Monday Kirby had not forgotten the court result. When he and Greg were having a cuppa in the office Kirby began whinging about how embarrassed he had been, and how he had thought about quitting, over the weekend.

He did not say anything about passing his assessment but Greg, having spoken to Murray over the weekend, already knew about the case. He also knew of the positive assessment. During the weekend conversation Murray had encouraged Greg to try to cheer the young officer up.

'Look,' said Greg. 'They reckon you're not really a prosecutor until you've lost a court case. I remember my first big loss and I know it's no fun. I can relate to how you are feeling but there is no need to think the world is about to end because you lost a case.'

Greg was off again. Perhaps this time his story telling was not just bragging but rather it had a legitimate, head office sanctioned purpose.

'You're not seeing the big picture. Remember the other day you were telling me about the bloke who rang up and told you the netters had caught all the fish. He based this on the fact he didn't get a bite and blamed us, if I remember right. Didn't he say something like, "Why don't youse blokes do something about the netting in Lake Mitagundi?"'

Greg didn't wait for a reply.

'Legitimate anglers deserve protection from illegal netters and they also deserve protection from the few complaining anglers who never seem to catch a fish. After an unsuccessful fishing trip it is all too easy to blame the activities of illegal netters or us useless inspectors.

'Often they ring up and complain, but when you ask if they can give more information, like a description of the vehicles or boat involved or the names of the offenders and where exactly the net is set, you get an answer like, "Oh, well, I don't exactly know, but everyone knows they're doin' it. All youse blokes 'ave to do is get off your bums and get on down there."

'Without a tip off, it is usually quite difficult to catch illegal netters. The culprits are frequently people who are legitimately in the area, often disguised as anglers. Many reported netters are nothing more than figments of imagination. Sorting the ghosts out from reality can be difficult. That's your problem at the moment, I reckon. The ghosts of the court case are muddling your thinking. Surely you know ghosts aren't real? Can't you see, losing one court case doesn't detract from the good job you are doing?

'Let me tell you about this case where I lost big time. One March, just after dark, I got just the sort of tip off needed. An angler, camped for a weekend's bream fishing became suspicious of another camp on the Saturday evening. It was a she as it turns out, and she said she had taken special notice and had seen a couple of fellows set a mesh net in the river. She gave me the location and a vehicle registration number.

'I rang Darren Wossfold and picked him up as arranged. We left for the nominated river late and it was close to midnight when we arrived. Despite the late hour, we looked up our informer and she pointed out the villain's camp and explained the location of the net she saw. She also suggested there may have been more than one net as the suspects spent some time well up the river near where it opens up into a long narrow lake.

'The suspect camp consisted of a caravan amongst some woolly tea-tree on the western side of the river. The net was supposed to be upstream from there, opposite a lone cypress tree in a paddock on the eastern side. Our information suggested the net had one end tied to the shore close to the tree. That was on the opposite bank and we had no boat!

'Our informer offered us hers but this meant we had to row past the offending camp. We accepted the offer and Darren carried out a reconnaissance mission to get the lay of the land in and around the caravan.

'It was well into the wee small hours and the suspects were sitting drinking around a blazing fire. Darren crept down through the tea-tree and crawled right under the caravan where he listened to their conversation. He returned after about a half hour having not heard anything coherent.

'He said he searched their boat as best he could in the dark and all he found were some spent cartridge cases, fishing rods and a bit of other angling stuff. After this reconnaissance we considered our handicap in having no motor on the boat wouldn't be too much of a problem. Those two were really into the beer and would have a hangover for sure. Besides, there was now a high expectation their outboard would perform to less than its potential. During the search of the boat Darren had somehow come upon the fuel mixture adjustment and idle screw on the motor. In the dark it was impossible for him to know exactly what happened!

'We launched our borrowed row boat, and as quietly as we could, made our way upstream. I don't think we really needed to worry. Those two had little chance of hearing us because of their excessive consumption of a certain amber fluid. It would have taken a lot more than a few squeaks from our oars to arouse their suspicion.

'We couldn't find the net and decided not to look for any others that may have been further up the river or in the lake. There may not have been any but if there were, a search would be a lot easier in daylight. We rowed up stream past where we thought the net should be and hid the boat in a patch of cane grass. We then walked back to the area near the cypress tree and looked for somewhere to hide ourselves.

'The ground between the tree and the river was open space, just a cow paddock and useless for a hiding place. The river created a virtual fence on one side of the paddock. The tree had a thin trunk and not one leaf or branch up to the height a cow could reach its tongue. Then we realised the cows, when milling around the tree for a bit of shade and a scratch, had caused a depression. The bare earth around the base of the tree was the best part of thirty centimetres lower than the surrounding paddock. Lying prone on our stomachs in the hollow we would be invisible from a boat in the river.

'So we settled down for the night on the bare earth in that depression. Well it was bare except for the cow dung, dry and wet!

'Dawn came, then sunrise. Nothing. There was no action until the sun was well and truly up and we were beginning to think our friends had detected us. Netters would never come and recover their gear in the brilliant sunshine that late in the morning.

Eventually we could hear the sounds of movement coming from the camp in the distance. During the launching of their aluminium boat, the suspects had caused a clunk and a bump or two that easily carried over the water. Then there was some good Aussie cussing as the motor failed to start. It eventually spluttered into life after a dozen or so pulls. The swearing continued all the way as the motor coughed and spluttered, under duress, pushing our netters upstream. I suspect the boat's occupants were operating on even less capacity than the motor, with its two cylinders more than just a little down on power!

'Disguised as cow pats, we made excellent observations as the boat headed straight past our location without so much as a look sideways. The only thing of interest was the considerable barrage of undeserved insults and threats directed at the makers of a particular brand of outboard motor. The abuse continued as the boat made a left-hand turn and disappeared from our view, travelling upstream to the lake.

'We recovered the row boat and followed. The river became narrow and winding, hedged in most places by quite tall cane grass. It eventually opened up into a bit of a lake and this is as far as we went. Remember this was a Sunday morning. Even though shooting on the Lord's Day was an offence back then, it was during the open duck season. The shotgun blasts coming from the top end of the lake were of little concern. We were concentrating on the netting. The shooting simply meant our friends were on a fishing and shooting weekend. Shooting on a Sunday was of no concern to us.

'We carefully chose the location of our ambush. A short distance downstream from the lake. Darren got out of the boat and into position in the cane grass. This was on the bank on a rather sharp left-hand bend. Downstream from there the river ran straight for about half the length of a cricket pitch before turning left again. I positioned the boat just around this second bend, the bow facing upstream. Darren had the anchor and rope from the row boat. From his hiding spot he could see any movement up the river to the lake and beyond. Our plan was foolproof.

'When the suspect craft eventually began to approach it was a simple matter for us to whisper advice and observations. Mostly this was pointless. Motor trouble had continued and the swearing had intensified. Before the netter's boat actually reached him, Darren stood up and shouted.

'"Fisheries Inspectors! Stop the boat!"

'The river was far too narrow to allow the men to turn the boat at that point and they kept going. When I heard the demand to stop I pushed the row boat forward and across the corner at my location. In that position, the borrowed row boat very nicely blocked the stream.

'By now Darren had everyone's attention. The abrupt and loud pronunciation of his request to stop diverted he crook's attention away from their downstream course. Our plan had been to surround these villains, me with the boat downstream and Darren, the moment they went past him, by throwing the anchor from his bank to the other, then holding the rope tight. I had my end sealed off beautifully but the execution of Darren's part in the ambush lacked a degree of finesse.

'As he stood up Darren put his foot amongst the coiled rope. When he threw the anchor, the rope tangled around his leg. With a great splash, the anchor landed about half way across the stream. Darren magnified the splash as he fell, sprawled in the shallows, very nearly over the drop-off into deep water.

'For some reason the suspects were not looking at me or the navigation hazard I presented. A collision imminent, I began to yell. I managed to grab the front of the boat and fend off the aluminium bow about to ram me amidships. Even with their motor performing so badly, such an encounter would have done some unwanted damage to our little borrowed row-boat.

'The two offenders were from a couple of neighbouring farms in the Western District if I remember right. Their only concern seemed to be we were about to seize their guns for shooting on a Sunday. They needed their firearms for vermin control, they said. We told them why we were there. You can guess, can't you? They were adamant they had not been netting, only shooting. As an afterthought they admitted to fishing the day before. Both had fishing licences.

'I'd already decided we would have a go in court on the basis of our civilian witness so I booked them up for netting the night before. I advised we had a civilian witness and bluffed we had a statement that even mentioned the cypress tree as the location of the net. In answer to several of my allegations, the ring-leader said, a couple of times, "The truth will come out." I thought this was some sort of nervous answer that didn't really mean anything.

'We let them leave and went looking for nets. We found none. When we got back downstream, their camp was gone but our witness was there waiting for the return of her boat. I took her statement and it was obvious she was more than happy to cooperate and come to court if necessary. I just thought she was a very keen angler especially unhappy about people who illegally set nets.

'Her only explanation for the net being gone was they must have recovered it the night before when she had left to make the phone call to inform me about it. On reflection, she said she did hear shooting from up the river the night before. "Yes," she said, "they may have been shooting but I didn't associate that with them. I'd seen one net and figured their time up the river was associated with more nets."

'Anyway when it came to the court case, our civilian witness was there with bells on. I spoke to the opposing solicitor, and guess what he said?'

Kirby did not know what he said.

'He said "The truth will come out," and I suppose it did.

'To cut a long story short, it turned out our civilian witness was the sister-in-law of one of the crooks and the other crook was also well known to her. The witness and her sister had grown up on the farm next door to where the brother-in-law lived. All four of them had gone to school together. They had even all gone fishing together as kids in the creek that separated the two farms. The girl's mother had died years before and our witness had left home to get a job straight out of school. The other sister had stayed home helping run the farm. She literally married the boy next door and over the years they both helped daddy run his farm. When the father also died, that's when things got ugly.

'It turns out, when both sisters and the husband were in the solicitor's office for the reading of the will it all blew up. And yes, it was the same solicitor who was conducting the defence in court. Daddy left the farm and absolutely everything in his estate to the sister. Our witness was not even mentioned in the will. She had apparently stormed out of the solicitor's office yelling, "I'll get you back for this."

'Under oath in the witness box she admitted the wretched family feud but insisted she had seen the net and her giving of evidence had nothing to do with her outburst about getting back at her sister and husband.

'The court was not so sure and dismissed all the charges, awarding costs against the prosecution.

'Like I said before, you shouldn't feel bad about your case. Look at the bigger picture. Murray told me no one could have won the case and you got an "A" for your assessment. Cheer up.'

Kirby felt better but he had to work at it.

Chapter 10

n September Greg went on leave. Kirby was acting officer in charge with no one as second in command. He enjoyed being his own boss and making decisions about work.

One Sunday morning he and Nicky were lying in bed when the telephone rang. When he answered Kirby recognised the voice of one of the local professional fishermen. He expected the call was to whinge about something. What better time to do this than on a Sunday morning when public servants should not be resting. Kirby had no idea he was about to meddle in international politics.

'You can even see the hammer and sickle on the chimney,' the caller advised as if this would somehow convey the truth and urgency of the situation.

Kirby realised he was listening to an eye-witness account.

'About midnight, on my way back to Mafeking Bay from the cape I heard radio chatter about a large Russian fishing trawler. I didn't give it much thought but right about daylight, I saw it. It was travelling east, south-easterly and I saw the warps leading off the stern. She was fishing, no worries, about ten nautical miles off shore, between the cape and here.'

Being of sound mind and an authorised Commonwealth Fisheries Inspector, Kirby recognised immediately the offence, if any, was a Commonwealth matter. The boat was outside the three mile limit of Victorian waters so he rang Melbourne and spoke to Murray

Stephens. Together they decided Kirby should charter a plane to try to locate the offending vessel. A short time later Kirby drove to the local airfield, and naively, took off in search of his biggest case ever. As they flew, Kirby imagined this was going to make Lincoln Campbell look like a small time crim.

The flight path crossed the coast between Costerfield and Mafeking Bay then travelled roughly parallel with the shore in passes beginning five nautical miles from land. During several runs back and forth, they saw nothing of interest. There just could not be a foreign fishing vessel within twenty-five nautical miles of the coast. Quite disappointedly Kirby told the pilot to head back to the airfield. Either the boat had hauled their nets and headed way out from land or the telephone information was incorrect or exaggerated.

As the plane turned, it was approximately twenty nautical miles south of the cape. The return flight was to take them to south of Mafeking Bay, then back over the coast not far from where they had crossed after taking off. Then, less than ten nautical miles off the coast they found the trawler! She was lying at anchor, not fishing.

'How the hell did we miss that before?' Kirby asked the pilot. He just shrugged.

Kirby felt indignant and personally violated. As the crow flew, this Soviet ship was not much over thirty-seven kilometres from his home. How dare they?

The pilot was very co-operative as Kirby took photos. The stall warning buzzer sounded constantly as he stood the plane on its wing, giving Kirby the best possible vantage point. On the deck Kirby could clearly see men, two hundred litre drums and what he thought was the net. Afterwards, when the photos were developed, it was possible to count the individual people and drums. Kirby was then positive there was a net but it was securely stowed and covered with a tarpaulin.

Kirby was excited and delighted. He had detected Victoria's first foreign fishing vessel. He was like a dog that had chased and caught a truck. Like the dog he had absolutely no idea what to do with his catch!

After the plane landed and Kirby had signed the invoice, he rang Murray again and told him breathlessly of the successful flight. Kirby then waited back home for Murray to ring back with instructions from Canberra. It was apparent Murray did not know what to do any better than Kirby. A couple of hours passed and Kirby continued to wait. His excitement turned to disappointment when the phone eventually did ring.

'Send in a detailed report in the next week or so and forget the boat. You might as well go back to having the day off.' This was really an instruction.

'But what are they doing about the boat?' Kirby demanded to know.

'I'm not sure,' said the boss. 'Canberra said they would send a telex to the Russian Embassy.'

Kirby was mystified. He could not believe it. He wondered why Canberra did not send a navy ship out to sink the boat. After all they were the enemy, or something. A month or so later an instruction came down the lines from Canberra. In future, all surveillance flights in relation to Commonwealth fisheries required specific prior approval from Canberra. Kirby never found out if Canberra did send a telex to the Russians.

Kirby related the story when Greg returned to work and was bemoaning how politics at all levels compromised their roles in conservation and fisheries management. Greg, not to be outdone in the story-telling department, totally changed the subject. Greg had his own political story and did not consider he had changed the subject at all.

'You know the department have created world history,' he said to Kirby. 'A few years back now the Federal Government placed a total ban on the import of all live salmonoids into Australia. They were concerned because of the threat of introducing an exotic disease. This means, over the years the feds have done some conservation work of value. Pity though they did not ban European Carp before 1961 when the Boolara Fish Farm imported them into Australia. But that's another story.'

Yes, it is another story, thought Kirby. *The first carp were intro-duced into New South Wales as early as the 1850's. The Boolara ones were not the first but they were probably the ones that caused the rapid expansion of carp and all their associated environmental damage and problems.* Kirby knew this from his studies but kept his mouth shut as Greg got on with his story.

'The salmonoid ban and the department's subsequent successful Chinook Salmon breeding program at Snobs Creek have both had significant political ramifications.

'In their natural range, Chinook Salmon live their adult lives at sea, returning to the river of their birth to spawn and die. The department became world famous when it managed to successfully adapt this cycle. The hatching of Chinook fry from brood stock that had spent their entire lives in fresh water was a world first.

'Hatchery bred fish became the basis of a successful recreational fishery in Lakes Purrumbete and Bullen Merri and in the day these lakes saw a higher than normal enforcement presence because of closed seasons as well as size and bag limits.

'Look, I know you can argue these two fisheries were artificial in that they were based on introduced species competing with native fish, but the opening of the salmon season at Purrumbete was a special event on the calendar for hundreds of anglers. Of course the politicians made hay and headlines, telling everyone how fantastic the government was because of the success of the whole program.

'In the week before the season opened, the department was most helpful to all the anglers. Several carefully chosen staff, yours truly included, spent a couple of days fishing at the lake, instructed to engage in research angling. It was all a political stunt but all of us who were involved loved fishing. With our specialist angling skills, we were then able to provide authoritative information to anglers who attended the opening. They all wanted to know the best lures and the best bait, how deep and how fast to troll, the best spots and a wealth of other information. It was all politics of course, designed to win votes at the next election. It had nothing to do with conservation or the protection of a natural resource or habitat. The department was anxious to cooperate and all us blokes loved every minute of it.

'The whole program was an enormous success. The minister of the day would invariably officially open the season with associated pomp and ceremony. Frequently a distress flare would signal starting time. That was an offence against the Marine Act but no one took any notice. Appropriate VIP guests and scores of reporters were always on hand. It's only natural for members of parliament to seek good publicity, and in this situation, what better publicity could there be than photos of the minister actually catching a salmon?

'And what more fitting boat could there be for a minister fishing on a calm water lake than a seven metre Shark Cat powered by twin two hundred horsepower outboard motors? Because only two people can troll comfortably out of a boat, even one as big as a Shark Cat, two such boats were obviously necessary. How else could the department demonstrate to the hosts of VIP guests they were actually important?

'Naturally ministers and their guests require the best of everything. Fishing supplies were purchased on government orders. This included brand new rods, reels, lures and line for everyone! There were also copious quantities of expensive food and liquid refreshments. Everything was ready and waiting when the official party arrived.

'Opening days always proved to be a wonderful success. The rivalry between the two departmental boats was good natured and made all the more amicable by generous proportions of good quality whisky. Naturally, those in the other boat had the good sense to let the minister win the fishing competition; such a conclusion being assured because of the constant progress reports being relayed between the boats via radio.

'At the end of the day, with photos taken and the press gone, the VIPs were standing on the end of the public jetty in the caravan park, sharing stories of their fishing adventures. The expression of individual success, experiences and joys of the outing sounded very much like everyone was talking in shorthand. By this time of night pretty much everyone involved had overdosed on tonsil varnish. It was pretty obvious many lacked normal human inhibition for shortly after the group began their yarns, one of the VIP's turned his back, walked a few metres and relieved himself. This performance took place on the end of the public jetty, right next to the departmental Shark Cat. As you know the official departmental logo and the words "Fisheries Patrol" are on the sides of our boats.'

Kirby acknowledged Greg had some skills in turning squalid politics into a funny narration, even if a few facts had been exaggerated. After a few moments merriment, Kirby had an additional thought. He expressed the view that his story far outweighed Greg's, simply on the basis of state versus international politics. Not to be outdone Greg simply reminded Kirby his story had international, national and state political ramifications. On that basis he declared himself the winner.

Although he had not expressed his story in the three political realms, Kirby considered he also had covered all three of the political tiers Greg claimed as proof of his victory.

Chapter 11

Just before Christmas Murray rang the office. In Greg's absence he spoke to Kirby. 'I'm doing some forward planning for next year and I want you to block out some time in your diary. If I remember right, you've had some experience down at Phillip Island with the mutton birds.'

Kirby remembered the trip. The minister's office had been getting complaints from the local tourism committee about mutton bird poaching. On that occasion Kirby had protested about having to go because Nicky was expecting their second child within a short time. With Phillip Island being an international tourist attraction, and pressure from the minister, those protests were unsuccessful. Kirby expected the same would apply now so kept his mouth shut.

'Sometime in the weeks leading up to Anzac Day the young birds will leave, so I don't want you making any commitments from late March till Anzac Day next year. I'm contacting other officers to make up a roster. You'll get five days away from Mafeking Bay, one to travel there, one to travel home and three day's duty on the rookeries. I'll let you know the exact dates when I've got the roster done. Have you already got commitments in that time?'

Kirby did not and he asked if the trip included Greg. It did not, just him. After the call was disconnected Kirby thought back to the previous trip. There are millions of the birds in question; Short-tailed Shearwaters. Tasmania has an open season and one could buy a licence to take them on a couple of Bass Strait islands. Again, he remembered the push last time to get a couple of scalps for the minister. The birds are an international migratory species and Phillip Island is an international tourist attraction. Kirby thought the politics of this proposal would be much the same as previously.

The breeding colony has a cycle that is as regular as clockwork. They lay their eggs at the same time, the young hatch at the same time and they migrate to sea at the same time. Near the end of their time on land the mutton-bird chicks are so fat they can't fly. The poachers only want these birds, and the precise nature of the breeding cycle is why this job could be scheduled so far in advance. The parent birds will have left and the young are easy to get in this time frame.

Naturally Kirby had a whinge or two to Greg in the months that followed but, in the end, his fate was sealed and the trip to Phillip Island eventuated. The first two nights on the rookery were uneventful. On the third night, despite the cold and drizzle, Kirby and his partner were both dozing off. In the small hours of the Thursday morning, both officers became conscious of voices. They glanced at each other and stared into the darkness, straining to see and hear. Within a few seconds the silhouettes of two people were visible. They walked in single file along the track leading through the rookery from the beach to the car park. The leading person carried a garbage bag.

Kirby and his mate had been hiding a few metres from the track and their interception involved little more than standing up, shining their torch-lights into the poacher's eyes and announcing their identities. Kirby emptied the garbage bag onto the ground and neither officer was surprised at the contents; two blood- smattered gloves and eight recently killed mutton birds. The evidence was incriminating but neither person said a word when interviewed. Kirby had been in this situation before and knew the law required him to "demand" names and addresses before the suspects were legally required to disclose them. Kirby took this to be simply the law making the distinction between an official request and a romantic solicit for the name and address of a female companion.

So demand names and addresses he did. Even with explanations of the law, and a second demand, the two men remained totally silent. They cooperated without a sound when Kirby requested they walk to the car park. As the procession left the end of the track a vehicle, with its lights on full beam, began to move in their direction. It suddenly swerved off course and roared away down the road.

'That wasn't your pick-up car by any chance?' Kirby asked.

By now both officers expected the silence that followed. Nothing Kirby tried convinced either of the two villains to say a thing. When threats of arrest failed, Kirby called the police on his mobile phone. Not long after the divisional van arrived Kirby's threats of arrest were put into effect.

Two prisoners, two police officers and two authorised wildlife officers were soon at the police station. There nothing changed. The police searched the men but found no identification. Apart from a grunt or two, when the duty sergeant asked the prisoners if they wanted to contact a friend or solicitor, there was no communication at all.

'Unless we know who you are, you will be remanded in custody and taken before court tomorrow morning,' the sergeant explained.

The bail justice gave an equally frank explanation of the consequences of remaining silent when the law required disclosure of names and addresses. Nothing worked. Next morning, after the prisoners had spent a night in the cells, the court called the department's case first and Kirby found himself explaining the story to the magistrate. He apologised for appearing without being in dress uniform. He began to give the details but was stopped and told to get to the nub of the matter.

'Why are these two in court when the court had no file related to them?'

Kirby pointed out they did not know who the defendants were; they had no identification, no vehicle and the Missing Persons Bureau was unable to assist.

'Despite extensive inquires during the previous night neither the police or departmental officers have been able to find out anything about these two men. In the circumstances I must oppose bail. My opposition would immediately disappear if the defendant's identities were known.'

Kirby sat down.

'You two are being extremely foolish.' The magistrate was addressing David Arnold and Raymond Bourke but no one knew their names yet. 'No doubt the police, the bail justice and the officers have been very patient with you. You are now in the big league and I give you fair warning. Wasting the court's time is not in your best interests. I have no option but to refuse bail and you will remain incarcerated until the authorities can determine who you are. Do you understand?'

'Can't you just give us a fine? This is extremely embarrassing. If our names get out we will have to quit our jobs and move interstate. Can't we just get this over and done with today?' David Arnold at last spoke.

Raymond Bourke nodded in agreement.

'If the officers agree, the court has time to hear your case today, later this afternoon when the normal list is completed,' the magistrate began. 'You have to understand though, the case cannot even be listed until you give your names and addresses to the officers. They then have to do some paperwork which has to be filed with the court. Are you now prepared to tell the officers who you are? If you are not, you will be back in the cells and there is no guarantee how long it may be before you get your next chance to go home.'

'Yes,' said Raymond Bourke.

This time David Arnold nodded.

The court formally remanded the two prisoners in custody and the police led them away. Kirby followed. Over at the station the officers interviewed the two men separately. Both Raymond Bourke and David Arnold gave their names and addresses, and despite there being no specific legal requirement to do so, they also provided their ages and dates of birth.

When questioned, they gave descriptions of their employment and explained what their homes physically looked like. In relation to the streets where they lived, they gave easy to follow directions on how to get there. They still had no formal identifications and the police rang the station closest to their homes in Nug Nug Upper.

The local policeman knew them both and vouched for their identities. He was not surprised the men did not want their names to become public in the circumstances. Both were local councillors who were seeking re-election at the polls to be held in a couple of weeks! Public knowledge of this affair would damage their chances. Kirby consulted the electoral roll and was satisfied as to their identities. Both spoke freely about the night before, and their stories were identical.

They had driven over to the island for a walk on the beach. During their outing they had found the mutton birds, already dead. Raymond Bourke had been carrying the bag and both defendants agreed he had picked up the carcasses. Both said he was about to dispose of them properly, into a bin. Both independently pointed out there had been a rubbish bin situated at the car park end of the track they were on.

'Phillip Island, being such a great tourist attraction and all, I thought dead mutton birds were bad for the image,' Raymond insisted.

'Just came over for a walk on the beach in the middle of the night. Conditions were good for walking last night, weren't they? Wet, raining and cold.' Kirby just couldn't help the sarcasm.

'Yes, that's right. We love walking in the wind and rain. We find it invigorating.'

'Just happened to have a garbage bag to put the mutton birds in, did we?' Kirby had just about had enough. He knew he would have to rest before travelling back to Mafeking Bay and that meant this five day trip was now at least six days long.

'Yes,' Raymond answered. 'I often find junk on the beach. It's disgusting what people leave lying about.'

'Just happened to have gloves with you too, I suppose. They wouldn't have been to protect your hands when you put them down the burrows would they?' Kirby was now being very sarcastic. He just could not help himself.

'No, actually they were just in my coat pocket. I didn't realise I had them till I put my hands in to keep them warm.' Raymond Bourke sounded offended. He put on a hurt puppy dog face.

'Give me a look at your hands,' Kirby demanded.

Raymond Bourke had scratches all over his. David Arnold had none and he stuck to his story.

'Listen mate, you've been told. I was there because I had been for a walk. You have no evidence I touched one of those stinking birds. The sight of them makes me sick. I was real glad when my nice friend, Raymond, started cleaning up the beach.'

Because of their stories, Kirby decided not to charge Raymond Bourke with killing the mutton birds. The alternative charge of possession better fitted the circumstances. He charged both with refusing to give their name and address.

In a little under five hours everyone was back in court and the defendants pleaded guilty. Kirby gave a summary of the previous night's events and the things said during the interviews. His production of the gloves as an exhibit very cleverly followed his word picture to the court. The blood was very obvious and the magistrate looked at them closely.

'I find the charges proven. Are there any prior convictions?' the magistrate seemed to speak as if by remote control.

'There is nothing known.'

'Is there anything either of you have to say about all this?' The tone of his voice now suggested he was listening. Kirby expected him to make some remark about the trouble they had caused and the obvious inference that could be drawn from the blood on the gloves.

Raymond Bourke responded first.

'I admit I had possession of the birds and that's why I pleaded guilty. But I want to explain that my actions last night were in response to my public duty. A lot of overseas visitors come to Phillip Island. The whole community benefits from tourism and we all need to do our bit. Cleaning up the beach is my contribution.'

'What about the gloves?'

Ah, Kirby thought, *the magistrate is listening.*

'Well, yes. I was going to explain about those. You see, earlier in the day I had been riding a trail bike through thick scrub and this was scratching my hands and forearms badly as it brushed past them on the bike controls. After some time the scrub was hurting so much I returned to my car and put on my coat and the gloves to protect myself. The blood on the gloves is mine, from my scratched hands. When I finished the ride I put the gloves into my coat pocket. When I went for the walk on the beach with my friend David I took my coat. The rest is exactly like I told the officers. I only remembered I had the gloves when I put my hands in my pockets to keep them warm.'

When the court asked David Arnold what he wanted to say, his reply was simple. 'Raymond has told you the story. I'm very sorry about all this.'

The court dismissed the possession charge as trifling and sentenced the two defendants to fifteen hours imprisonment on the charge of failing to give their name and address. The defendants were immediately released because of the time already spent in custody. Outside Kirby was livid.

'Those two were both poaching mutton birds,' he said. 'The older one wore gloves and that's why he had no scratches. That business about the motor bike in the bushes is all rubbish. And I bet the magistrate recognised their names as being on the local council. That's why he dismissed the possession charge as trifling.'

Kirby had no proof at all about the magistrate recognising the names but he was upset and letting off steam. As he and his partner walked towards their car, he suddenly stopped.

'Look at this,' he said holding up two right hand gloves. 'I knew the motorbike story was as genuine as the rubbish collection one. They were poachers like I knew all along but it's too late now.'

It was also too late to begin the trip back to Mafeking Bay.

Chapter 12

The following Monday when Kirby and Greg were part way through discussing the work plans for the week Greg lost interest in what needed to be done. Somewhat typically he revisited personal, past accomplishments.

'I've been thinking about catching netters after we discussed the court case I lost when the truth came out. There was another time when I nearly lost a case. Well actually, I nearly didn't get the case so I suppose it means I nearly lost in court, doesn't it?

'I think I've told you before about a few of the feuds between departmental research staff and us enforcement officers. After numerous in-house quarrels a departmental policy was developed. It established our research netting protocols. I have told you, haven't I?'

Greg did not wait for Kirby to reply. 'Without the policy, enforcement staff sometimes failed to see past the letter of the law and the research scientist and their technical assistants failed to see what the fuss was all about. Testing the integrity of the policy was all in a day's work back then.

'I remember one of the technical assistants working on a research project. He was studying the distribution of Estuary Perch and Australian Bass. As required by the policy, he rang early one week and provided details of his netting schedule. This was to begin at dusk the following Sunday in the lower reaches of one of our rivers.

I just forget the schedule but that doesn't matter. What matters is the schedule saw nets in one river one night, the next river the next night and so on until the Thursday evening when the nets were to be set for the last time before they were pulled on the Friday morning. After that, the research blokes would return to Melbourne. I just made a mental note and forgot about it; that is until the telephone rang at home the next Monday night.

'"Someone has just put a net in the Sturt River. Are they allowed to do that?" the woman asked.

'"No madam, they are not. Can you please tell me exactly where the net is?"

'"Well they put the boat in at the boat ramp on River Parade, the first one, the one near where it turns into Carr Street. They went virtually straight across from there, perhaps down a bit towards mouth, then up a little inlet that branches off the main river."

'I know exactly where that is. Thank you very much.

'That was about the first time in my whole career where someone gave me directions I could follow precisely. This impressed me so much I forgot to ask for my caller's name and contact number. I even forgot to ask for a description of the vehicle and boat involved, or even how many people she had seen.

'I was gearing up for another all-night stint when I remembered the research program for bass and perch. It can't be, they netted there last night, didn't they? I thought. I was trying to convince myself. Tonight they are in one of the inlets down towards the lighthouse, aren't they? I wished I had made a proper note rather than relying on memory. I didn't know whether to go or just forget the darned net. I procrastinated while the jug boiled, then decided I had to go.

'As I left on my way to the net, I continued to debate with myself. Was this the official research netting or not? By the time I arrived, I had convinced myself I was chasing the department's own research staff. If I remembered their schedule correctly, and this was the research assistant who had phoned me, I was going to demonstrate my qualifications from the Pol Pot School of Diplomacy. There was no doubt I was in a real good mood to catch a technical assistant.

'I launched the boat and hid the departmental car by simply leaving it parked in the driveway of one of the houses nearby. It looked like an upmarket sort of holiday house or weekend retreat. Being a Monday night and all, I guessed the owners were away and hoped they wouldn't arrive home that night.

'I motored the short distance across and down the river then turned up the inlet the lady told me about. As large as life, there was a massive white buoy floating for the world to see. I lifted it clear of the water. Sure enough; it marked the location of a nice new set of square hooks.

'Not too concerned about hiding, I pulled the boat in beside a clump of mangroves, made myself as comfortable as possible and tried to sleep. By midnight the departmental netting research blokes were not my favourite people. I can't begin to tell you the things I thought about them, and I had several hours to work up my aggravation. By first light next morning, when I heard the motor of an approaching boat, I had firmly resolved I was not going to be sending them Christmas greetings. I had just spent about eight hours sitting in a four metre boat I could not get out of because of the mud and the mangroves!

'It was about this time I realised the tide was right out and I was well and truly aground on the mud. A few seconds after this revelation I realised the two people in the approaching boat were real live netters, not departmental research staff at all.

'The suspects saw my boat a short distance before they reached the net. In surprise they stopped to look at me in the half light. We were not more than ten or fifteen metres apart and those pirates just could not believe their eyes. There was a bloke in a boat, sitting by the end of their net. I wanted to but could not make it across to them because of a certain lack of water at my end of the journey. There was nothing I could do except speak to them.

'Nice morning, gentlemen. Greg Bayliss is my name. I'm a fisheries inspector. Best bring your boat over here, I think.

'I don't know why, but they did. The person driving was a professional fisherman who lived nearby and the other person was his brother-in-law. Perhaps the professional recognised me and assumed I already knew his identity. I didn't. He was wearing a beanie and I didn't recognise him until he came right across to my private mud.

'The professional was okay, real good actually. He helped me get out of the mire, waited while I hauled the net and then truthfully answered all my questions. At the end of it all, I finished with the usual statement of the law and gave them the opportunity of telling me why. You know how it goes; "it is an offence to use a mesh net in inland waters. What is your excuse for setting this net here last night?"

'"Well," he said, "I was down here the night before last and I saw your research blokes. They told me they were netting for Estuary Perch and Australian Bass here and down the coastal creeks and rivers and all. I figured if I put a net in the same place, everyone would think it was still them."

'This matter will be reported. Is there anything else either of you wish to say about it?' I concluded the interview hoping the men would not detect my disappointment. Anyway, we won the court case. They pleaded guilty and you're the first person I've ever told about my true feelings that night.'

Kirby was about to get back to the work planning but Greg had other ideas. He had caught a netter or two in his time.

'Now that I'm in the mood for truthful stories, there was another time I got the netter but things didn't really go according to plan. Well, we sort of got the netter. It's a bit of an embarrassment really.

Anyway, I figure you'd better hear it from me rather than the version they undoubtedly tell down the pub.

'This all happened out on the east side of Lake Mitagundi. As normal, you usually get a netting case because of a tip off. That's what happened and the info was spot on. I rushed out there in the car, not knowing who I was trying to catch. When I got to the spot though, I did know I was looking for a boat. How do you reckon I knew that?'

Kirby did not know.

'It was obvious wasn't it? The net was out in deep water.'

'It wasn't obvious to me anymore than its obvious how you knew it was a net if you went out to the lake by car and the net was in deep water. Did it have a sign on it?' Kirby was getting a bit frustrated with Greg. He thought he was boasting and at the same time, trying to belittle Kirby by asking him questions he had no hope of answering. Besides he knew the weekly planning wasn't finished and the form still had to be completed and sent off to head office. Greg's story-telling was a waste of time.

'Well, I then had to find a place to hide, didn't I?' Greg did not seem to be aware of Kirby's exasperation. He appeared equally unconscious of the need to get on with real work that had to be completed in a short time. Greg just went on with his story as if he did not hear or understand Kirby's additional frustration at the lack of detail in the story.

'The only thing on the shore at that spot was a rusty old tin bathtub that was lying just the right distance from the net to make a good observation post. From behind the bath I had an excellent look-out and no chance of detection by anyone in a boat on the water near the net. Again I waited all night and no one came. Just before dawn, a bloke called David Hughes arrived by car, and my planning appeared to be fatally flawed.

'Luckily the car headlights did not shine directly at me and somehow I managed to remain hidden. You wouldn't believe it. Hughes used the bath as a boat! He just dragged it over to the water and launched it. He had a canoe paddle that he used and out he went to the net, just like that. It had a buoy on both ends and I suppose I was only guessing it was a net until he hauled it into his make-shift boat.

'I then just waited until he returned to shore with the evidence in the bath. At the time the strategic advantage of my hiding place was unquestionable, but for a while there it was touch and go.'

'Where was your car hidden? How come he didn't see you? Where did you hide when he came over to the bath?' Kirby wanted to know all these details but Greg did not think they were important. He thought it was equally unimportant to answer his junior officer.

'Well, introductions were unnecessary because this was not the first time I'd had dealings with Hughes. I had his name and address in my memory for a similar indiscretion about a year before. That time he was using a tinny the court ordered forfeit.

'Anyway, when my official questions began, Hughes had a severe case of post interception depression. As you can gather, he was a bit of a pirate, and for some reason his usual bravado and rhetoric were all gone. His answers were quiet and truthful and included an admission he intended to sell the fish he'd illegally caught that morning.

'I was on a roll. Previous stories about fish sales in local pubs became specific questions about other illegal netting. In a dozen or so questions I had notes on Hughes's additional netting spots and the sales outlets for his illegally taken fish.

'When the offence file arrived back for prosecution, the charges included a hamburger with the lot. There were several charges for netting in prohibited waters. For each of these there were corresponding charges of illegally taking fish for sale. Someone had also decided to test the legal definition of "boat" which, as you know, means "any means of transportation on water." This definition formed the basis of a charge for using an unregistered boat. The hamburger with the lot charges also related to no life jacket, no bailing bucket and failing to display navigation lights.

'Hughes pleaded guilty to each charge in court. But that's not the end of the story.'

Kirby felt sure Greg heard his frustrated sigh.

'Hughes did not stop his illegal netting and I blame the weak sentence handed down by the court on that particular occasion. They didn't even forfeit the bathtub, even though they found the unregistered boat charge proven. After all, Hughes already had a couple of prior convictions for this sort of offending.

'Anyway, the next time Hughes was caught netting, Darren Wossfold was involved when I was on leave. Darren had a young officer from Melbourne with him. As I understand the story, it involved another good tip off from the public and again two buoys marked the ends of the net.

It was out at Lake Mitagundi again. Like always with netters, it was an all night wait and again the officers did not know who the offender was. It was winter. To remain warm throughout the night the officers were wearing civilian clothing. Unfortunately this proved to be a crack in their armour. Hughes subsequently seized upon it.

'Neither officer had met Hughes before that night. When he arrived, just as dawn was beginning to lighten the eastern sky, his girlfriend was with him in the car. She remained seated in the car when Hughes walked over to end of the net tied to some vegetation on the shore. As he began to haul the net, the officers walked up to intercept. Both produced identification cards and Hughes went berserk, king-hitting Darren with a well-aimed fist to the face.

'From that moment, half our enforcement team were on sick leave and it didn't take long for the second officer to join the ranks of the wounded in action. He approached the car Hughes had arrived in and wrote down the registration number. He then attempted to find other clues as to the identity of the offender. He started to open the vehicle door to search it. He didn't know anyone else was there but as he put his hand on the door, Hughes grabbed him by the shoulder and spun him round. The severe impact of Hughes's knee in the inspector's groin sent the officer collapsed to the ground, totally crippled.

'In retrospect we think the aggression displayed by Hughes on that occasion was more characteristic. Perhaps I was lucky on the previous times I had dealings with him because he gave me no trouble. Maybe his aggression developed over the years, or it could have had something to do with his girlfriend being there. We don't really know.

'After, when they were physically able, the officers withdrew and reported the incident to the police. By then Hughes and his girlfriend were gone and the boys in blue referred the case to the CIB. They were most eager to assist as they knew Hughes because he had quite a criminal history with the police as well as all his priors with us. His police prior convictions included a few for serious assaults and one of his recent victims was his girlfriend!

'Anyway, when the fisheries prosecution file was processed in head office, there were telephone conversations between the department and the police to coordinate both prosecution actions.

'The police charged Hughes with two counts of assault causing actual bodily harm. They also charged him with recklessly causing seriously injury. On their advice head office did not lay charges of assault under the Fisheries Act. The police were adamant their charges were more appropriate because they carried higher penalties. With his police record for similar offences, Hughes would get a sentence of imprisonment for six months. At least six months, they said. When our file arrived with me for prosecution, it contained charges for illegal netting only.

'On the police charges, Hughes elected to have a trial by a judge and jury in the county court. The magistrates' court adjourned our netting charges until after the higher court concluded the case involving the assaults under the Crimes Act.

'At the trial, Hughes claimed he did not know the identity of the two people who had come abruptly at him out of the darkness.

"One of them held out a credit card," he claimed. "They were telling me they had me. I thought they were going to rob me of my credit cards and money. I had to protect myself. I was frightened. They were not in uniform and they did not say who they were. Sure I hit one but only in self-defence. After that, the other one went over to my car and started to touch up my girlfriend. I had to protect her and that's why I kneed him in the groin. He was not going to have his filthy way with her."

'Darren and I were both in court and I could not believe it when the jury returned a verdict of not guilty and the judge dismissed all the police charges.

'Eventually the magistrates' court found the netting charges proven and the list of convictions and fines against Hughes grew a bit longer. I think he stopped netting after that. At least departmental intelligence ceased to mention his name in despatches concerning people of interest.'

Chapter 13

'We are up to Wednesday afternoon on the planner. What are we doing for the rest of the week?' At last Kirby could get on with his relationship with FRED and his insatiable appetite for paperwork.

The following afternoon, the two officers were following the weekly planner and were writing briefs in the office. A sudden telephone direction from head office had them rush off on an unscheduled assignment. Instead of paper work, they were now supposed to be checking shark catches being unloaded from professional fishing boats in port.

Kirby was beginning to wonder at the frequent head office reminders telling of their obligation to submit their weekly forward plans via FRED. These documents were frequently inaccurate and head office must understand. *Perhaps, Kirby supposed, the people who see the forward plans do not see the diary copies. The two documents show no resemblance to each other; one being based on forward plans or dreams and the other on past facts. And today's changes are typical! We do our planning and are then directed to do something else.* Kirby was beginning to sympathise with Greg's delinquent attitude towards the persistent paper warfare needed to fuel the bureaucracy.

They arrived at their favourite lookout over the harbour where the professional fishing boats tied up, unloaded, refuelled and moored. Here they waited for the first of the boats to arrive and begin unloading. As the afternoon wore on, Kirby became increasingly annoyed as he thought about his untouched paperwork while they sat on their butts doing nothing.

'What's with the shark ban anyway?' he asked Greg.

'It all began in the early 1970's' Greg explained. 'Victoria introduced a maximum size limit for two species of shark. From then on it's been an offence to possess gummy and school shark that are too big. That's in addition to the law about undersize. These fish are carnivores at the end of the biological food chain. Consequently their flesh contains mercury in concentrations above World Health Organisation recommended limits.

'The introduction of this ban had human health concerns associated with eating fish with too much mercury in the flesh. The heavy metal is of special concern to pregnant women and the under-privileged. Scientists advise this second group is at extra risk because of their frequent ingestion of flake as part of their regular Friday night meal of fish and chips.

'Anyway, Victoria is the only place in Australia where the ban applies and it didn't take long for a black market in illegal shark to develop. Shark flesh, or flake, is Victoria's preferred fish in the traditional feed of fish and chips and this reflects in the black market price. The black market price here is higher than the price for any sort of shark in the other states, with the exception perhaps of Tasmania. That's probably on a par with Victoria because the Taswegians love their flake, too.

'Many people argue, me included, that the mercury in our shark is organic and not harmful like the industrial mercury that did cause horrible sickness in Japan. Our politicians can't see that though. All they see is a few votes as they spruik about mercury that caused severe poisoning in Japan. Villagers ate fish contaminated with mercury from a factory discharging waste into a bay. The Victorian industry generally does not accept the reason for the law and I for one, hate doing work that should be done by the Health Department. You mark my words; this law will be repealed before too long. In the meantime we have to do what we are told.'

After several unproductive hours sitting, watching, waiting and belly-aching, a professional shark fisherman named Bradford Collins arrived in the port with a hold full of illegal shark. Greg and Kirby did not know about the shark for sure but they knew he was a shark fisherman and therefore a prime suspect.

They also knew from the moment it became known they were keeping surveillance on a shark boat, the local folk, especially fishermen and those in the industry, would fire up their various grapevines. Soon marine radios and telephones would broadcast the unambiguous message: "The seagulls are in town."

For this very reason, officers were officially issued with a second set of vehicle number plates. Kirby had put these on the departmental F100 utility before they left the office.

It was winter time and darkness set in early. The officers parked past the boat ramp where recreational fishers frequently left vehicles while they angled. Here they hoped to blend in as tourists who were fishing.

It was now after dark. Only upon a very close inspection by someone in the know would their vehicle be recognised. As they began discussing their best chance of a successful interception, a vehicle arrived and pulled up on the jetty beside the shark boat. Two men clambered off the boat with some luggage they bundled into the car boot. They then climbed into the car and it left the area. The boat sat at the unloading wharf, unattended for over two hours.

Greg and Kirby expected their presence had been detected and broadcast but felt sure the boat would contain illegal shark. They decided to sit it out. They discussed the fact that, so late at night in a relatively small coastal town they must have been detected. If so they were wasting their time. They were entertained for a short time by a romantic couple engaged in private business in a car parked a short distance away.

Just as Greg was contemplating calling it quits a utility towing a tandem trailer arrived at the un-loading bay. A second vehicle stopped up near the fishing co-operative and a person began to walk toward where they were parked. This was a most indirect route from the co-operative to where Collins had berthed. In the circumstances the officers were now certain they were about to be discovered.

By that hour of the night there was only one other vehicle left parked in the area where the officers were. Their feelings of exposure and vulnerability were certainly based on sound evidence. The romance emanating from the other car gave the officers an idea. They agreed if the pedestrian came too close, they would have to pretend to be an item too and cuddle up to make it look real. Kirby was very relieved when he did not have to act out this charade; Greg had a beard and Kirby knew he would have had to play the girly part.

The shadowy figure walked close to the other car and seemed to glance at their number plate. It then turned and walked back in the direction of the co-operative. If the visitor had walked closer to the official vehicle and checked it out thoroughly, Kirby doubted his acting would have passed the test.

Shortly afterwards, car lights moved from the co-operative down to the boat where three people set to work unloading shark carcasses. Kirby and Greg watched. Some went straight into the rear of the utility and some went onto the trailer. After counting about thirty shark bodies off the boat, they made their move. As they arrived, feeble attempts to cover up the activities were unsuccessful.

Collins obviously knew the law. While Kirby and Greg were still making an assessment of the situation Collins told them he knew the score.

'I know what youse blokes'll do. You've got ideas about seizing me fish, don't ya?'

'We have to measure them; any that are oversize will be kept aside from your legal catch. We can talk about what will happen when we finish inspecting the shark.'

'Don't crap on,' Collins replied. 'You're gonna seize 'em and if you think we're gonna help unload, then you've got barnacles for brains. To save you the hassle though, all them what's in the port freezer are legal. You don't have to look at them. I'm having another beer. You should have them unloaded by about one or half past. See ya then.' Collins disappeared into the cabin and called his two helpers after him. One was his younger brother Louis.

It was very cold, hard work in the freezer. As the officers did not have appropriate clothing, they took turns down below. Collins reappeared on the deck after twenty minutes or so. He was drinking directly from a long necked beer bottle. Kirby guessed it was his second since he has left them to the unloading.

When Collins reappeared, he also had an old Harrington and Richardson single barrel, twelve-gauge shotgun. This was just a little off-putting. When Collins started tapping the barrel of the gun on the hand rail outside the cabin door, Kirby and Greg had some diffi-culties concentrating on the shark.

'Ya know,' Collins drawled. 'I think I'd use this on youse buggers, but I'm scared if I pulled the trigger this old bitch might blow up and kill me, too.'

Collins continued to tap the barrel on the rail. As he did the wooden fore-end fell off the gun and dropped over the side into the water between the wharf and the boat.

That splash was a welcome relief and very much preferable to the sound of a shotgun blast! Not even Collins would have used the gun without the fore-end. He placed it back into the cabin and continued to suck on the beer bottle. When it was empty, he threw it over the side.

'I ain't got no more beer. Youse blokes got any beer?'

The officers assured him they did not.

'I'm going up the street to get some more. Come on.'

He beckoned his crew and they all soon left the wharf in the second vehicle.

Kirby was positive they were not going to be able to legally buy beer at that hour. Greg was positive this may be their one opportunity to call in the cavalry. Collins had become less than rational the more he drank. After a short discussion, Greg took the government car and went in search of police help. When vehicle lights started approaching less than ten minutes later, Kirby's anxiety doubled. When he saw Greg was in the car, he stopped worrying.

'I got Jackie Blewitt out of bed,' Greg explained. 'She'll be here just as soon as she puts her uniform on and signs out her revolver and ammunition.'

Collins arrived shortly afterwards carrying a dozen large bottles of beer in an unopened carton. He became more aggressive as he continued his alcohol intake. When the police car arrived not long afterwards there was a remarkable change in his demeanour. He may have realised the police were there as a result of a request for help, but Kirby doubted it. He suspected the alcohol would have already had a considerable negative effect on the functioning of brain cells. The significance of the blue uniform, however, still penetrated to the control room of his behaviour.

All the illegal shark were finally off the boat and loaded into the rear of the departmental utility. Having been frozen the fish did not re-stack well. The rear of the truck was absolutely full with shark carcasses hanging out over the lowered tailgate. The weight of the load was such the front wheels had very little steerage as Kirby drove up off the unloading bay.

Next morning Greg arranged to take the seized shark out to sea in the public works boat, the Sand Piper. She was an ex-navy work boat and very, very solid. After Kirby and Greg loaded all the contraband onto the work boat, they boarded and she steamed out of the harbour with the public works skipper at the helm.

Collins knew what was going on, probably as a result of the local grapevine. He followed in his shark boat and as they steamed around the bay in a large arc the officers dumped the carcasses overboard, one or two at a time.

The Sand Piper was slightly the faster boat but as Collins' boat took the smaller arc, it managed to keep pace. When the last of the shark disappeared over the side, and the work boat was approaching the harbour entrance, it seemed for a minute or two there may have been a dead heat. The Sand Piper eventually rounded the end of the sea wall first and made its way back to the wharf and its normal berth.

As it came along side, all concentration was on the task of tying up and nobody was watching Collins. Suddenly someone yelled out and Kirby looked up to see the shark boat steaming down on the Sand Piper. It rammed the workboat, bow first to the port side, amidships. Collins did throw the fishing boat into reverse just before impact but displacement boats that size take a considerable time to stop.

A piece of wood about a metre long broke right out of the bow of the fishing boat as it collided with the reinforced side of the Sand Piper. Several of the planks on both sides of the bow also sprung and she was now in a very unseaworthy state. The work boat had a very small dent in her metal gunwale and a scrape on the paint work.

With not one word from her skipper, the shark boat reversed away from the point of impact and steamed over to its normal mooring. Here Collins leant over the bow and inspected the damage. Someone from the Sand Piper yelled across the harbour inviting the fisherman to participate in another race, but this time directly into the swells in Bass Strait. Lying in the calm waters of the harbour, the shark boat was in no immediate danger but there was no doubt she would not go to sea again without considerable and expensive repairs.

In court several months later Collins explained he had previously been having trouble with the gear box and the collision occurred when he could not get his boat into reverse! His solicitor produced to the court a receipt for repairs to the gear box and for repairs to the bow of his boat.

It puzzled Kirby why the gearbox receipt had the date smudged to the point it was illegible. The defendant avoided any explanation for following the Sand Piper in the first place and made no comment for his possession of the illegal shark. The court also had some difficulty in excusing the defendant's behaviour and it proceeded to convict and fine him heavily.

After the court case, the next week's work plan included a coastal patrol to the thirty-two mile reef. As the name suggests, this was thirty-two nautical miles off shore from the lighthouse. When the plan was discussed and submitted on the Monday, Kirby and Greg had decided this patrol had no specific mission just a general tour of duty designed to fly the flag. As the whole venture was dependent on weather and sea conditions the work plan included a caveat to that effect. It was Wednesday before the weather bureau suggested conditions would be suitable on Friday morning.

While the range of the patrol boat was sufficient for the return trip, even taking into account the distance from the bay to the lighthouse, this would be a big day. It was the first time such a trip had been considered and the officers reasoned no one would be expecting them so far from base.

After launching before daylight, they made their way out through the entrance just on daylight in the middle of December. By the time the sun rose they were well underway, steaming down the coast on a beautiful day. As prearranged they stopped and made radio contact with a third officer who was on short-term assignment to help. It was only this additional assistance that made the long trip feasible from an OH&S perspective. He was in the works utility towing the boat trailer. The fact the vehicle and trailer were not at the boat ramp had also been part of the planning. The locals would know this was where the official vehicle and boat trailer were always left during any official fisheries patrols.

The vehicle driver kept well behind the patrol boat so as not to compromise any surprise the boat may have had so far from its base. All the way down the coast the officers found not one boat to surprise.

After their journey down past the lighthouse and out to the reef, they were travelling back towards Mafeking Bay when they saw a professional shark boat half a mile ahead. It was also headed towards the bay and Greg recognised it as the boat normally skippered by Bradford Collins. It was inside the three nautical mile limit of Victorian waters.

While it was only a little over a week since the court case, it had been well over six months since the previous encounter when the officers had seized oversize shark from this boat. Today the work plans had not had any particular person or even a particular fishery in mind. It was just that Collins and his shark boat were the first opportunity for an interception and inspection on the trip.

The patrol boat easily caught the slower displacement vessel. With the Shark Cat almost riding its wake like a surfer, Kirby virtually stepped off the bow and on to the shark boat's stern quarter.

This surprise attack was almost too good. Fishermen who have been at sea for a couple of days usually know precisely the number of people on their boats. Kirby tapping at the wheel house window way out at sea was almost too much for Bradford and Louis.

When the shark boat stopped Greg tied to a couple of starboard bollards and joined Kirby. The Collins brothers had about twenty oversize school shark in the hold and Kirby smiled inwardly, feeling pretty pleased the long trip had been worthwhile. These pirates had prior convictions for the exact same offence.

The fishermen had an ingenious excuse that really came as no surprise. They claimed their possession of the illegal shark had a legitimate goal. Their sale would not benefit them personally but rather all the proceeds would be paid to a benevolent fund established for the spouse of a local fisherman. The officers were aware of the circumstances where Joe Johnson, one of their local fishermen, had recently lost his life. He had overturned his boat in very rough seas as he navigated the rip leading into Mafeking Bay. The tragedy had touched the entire fishing industry in the area.

Kirby realised this story would make excellent plea material in court. He figured a more generous gesture would have been a contribution from legal activities. When he robbed from the rich, Robin Hood always intended to give to the poor but that did not alter the fact, his actions were illegal.

On this occasion, the needy widow may have been behind the fishermen's intentions but the illegal shark had to be seized. Kirby relayed this fact to both the fishermen. Based on the previous experience when he has seized shark from Collins, Kirby expected an unfavourable reaction to this news. He got one but not the one he expected.

Bradford understood the officers had a job to do and he was not affected by alcohol. He was perfectly reasonable and this surprised Kirby. It did not surprise him though as much as the reaction from Louis. When he heard the news his response was to appeal to the very basis of the officer's humanity.

'How could you do this to the poor widow? Have you no feelings at all? You knew Joe, didn't you? Surely you can see this is a legitimate case? We are not doing it for us! We are only doing it out of the goodness of our hearts.'

Kirby and Greg argued two wrongs did not make a right. They spoke of the dangers to the health of the general community but this logic only inflamed the situation. The Collins brothers were well versed in the difference between industrial mercury poisoning and the organic mercury that was supposed to be the problem in Victoria.

The officers got a lecture, not only on the differences between organic and industrial mercury, but also the stupidity of the law. This finished and Kirby expected they could get on with the business and finalise the note taking. Louis had other ideas. He had only just begun.

'These few sharks will make no difference to the health issue, not that there is one, but they will make a difference to a very worthy cause. Look, it's nearly Christmas. Have you two got no feelings at all?'

His plea for compassion did not work and the tone of the supplication changed as he made several remarks about the officer's inhumanity.

'If you two were human, but I doubt you are, then you're certainly at the lower end of the evolutionary scale.'

Lewis still had a move or two. His next tactic was passion. He began to cry. With real tears in his eyes he grasped the boat's mast near where they all stood. He wailed and circled around, sometimes falling down on his knees in desperation. As a fisherman and mate of the dead man, he could not willingly be party to such a heartless decision. In the circumstances he would probably have to take his own life. This was just all too much for Kirby. Still with tears rolling down his cheeks, Lewis began to monkey up the mast, advising he had decided what he must do.

'I can't live with myself being part of this. The only honourable thing to do is finish it now.'

This was as disconcerting for Bradford as it was for Kirby and Greg. The skipper's soothing voice and reassuring words at last began to work. His big strong hands, clasped firmly around his brother's ankle, helped too. The distressed man finally calmed down, came down and went below deck to have a little lie down.

Kirby knew he and Greg would discuss their proposed course of action on the boat trip home. He was sure they would still have to report the matter to head office but, at his suggestion, it was the skipper who threw the offending carcasses over the side.

Next week, when they were back in the office, the officers submitted the usual report of the alleged offence. No legal proceedings, or even a letter of warning, followed.

A few months later the law banning oversize shark was repealed.

Chapter 14

Whenever Kirby was melancholy, his mind often wandered to three malignant and unfinished work episodes. This dejected feeling occurred more and more frequently, especially when even the smallest of things did not work out as he expected or hoped.

Firstly, he remembered his confrontation with Lincoln's lady friend outside court on the day the court had cancelled Lincoln's crayfish licence. He remembered, too, the horrific telephone calls and the pending court case instigated by the police. It seemed this millstone would be hanging around his neck forever.

Secondly, he remembered the Victorian Supreme Court writ that personally claimed damages against him, the other officers and the State of Victoria in relation to his part in the seizure of the Shark Cat in South Australia. These thoughts invariably conjured up the extent of damages that may be claimed by a professional abalone diver who had been deprived of his income for a year or so. Kirby's imaginary money amounts were very alarming.

Thirdly, Kirby had not forgotten he was still owed the last laugh in relation to Lincoln's abalone poaching. While Kirby had been involved, perhaps even instrumental in the apprehension of Lincoln early in his work at Mafeking Bay, it appeared any proper punishment seemed to be avoided through a court system that allowed appeals on appeals.

Despite Kirby's negative attitude that it would take forever for the "threats to kill" court case to be finalized, it was eventually listed for hearing. To everyone's surprise Lincoln's lady friend entered pleas of guilty to all charges! Consequently Kirby did not have to attend court or give evidence. The determination of the court was quite appropriate, having an element of punishment, rehabilitation and protection. On one charge the court imposed a $3,000 good behaviour bond. This was in relation to the Victorian Crimes Act. A condition of the bond was that Lorren Bibby was prevented from making any contact with Kirby for five years from the date of the hearing. A second five year good behaviour bond was imposed on a second Victorian charge. This was the same charge but on a different date. The remainder of the charges, including the Commonwealth ones, were adjourned for the same five years. "After this time", the court explained, "if you do not get in any more trouble these matters will be dismissed. If that happens you will not have to pay the $3,000."

After he was told of the result the number of times Kirby felt melancholy lessened by a third.

Chapter 15

During their forward planning meeting on the next Monday, Kirby and Greg discussed the fact they had not done any work on Lincoln Campbell for quite a few months. They discussed this in light of the fact there had been a couple of pretty strong rumours about his continued illegal fishing for abalone all the time.

'I'll bet he is still active. It's just that over the years he's become even more difficult to detect.' Greg lowered his voice even though there was no one except Kirby in the office. 'I haven't told you this before but there is some info to suggest there is a possible leak from within the department. I've been discussing this awful thought with head office. They want us, that is you and me, to come up with an operational plan for when our Fisheries and Wildlife Officer's annual conference is on next month. No one else will to be told a thing but you and I will not be going to the meeting in Swan Hill. The only other officer in the know is Murray Stephens. Unless otherwise specifically arranged, I will be the only person to discuss this with him. That means I am the only person in the world you can discuss this with.'

'What about Nicky?'

'At the moment leave it as if we are going to Swan Hill for the conference. There is less risk of an accidental leak that way. We are to prepare an operation plan to correspond with the week of the conference. I'll liaise with Murray.'

In this context, the officers secretly planned a mission. With the knowledge of only one other officer, they set a trap to be sprung during the conference week. Kirby and Greg would pretty much be working alone but the operation plan did incorporate the potential for police support when and if they were successful. The plan did not go so far as advising the police about the conference. The basic hypothesis was to capitalise on the element of surprise, and the assumption there was a leak. That leak, it was hoped, would advise Lincoln all officers were attending the annual get-together of all departmental enforcement officers, and they were all well out of the way, up north for a week. If by chance he learned Kirby and Greg were absent from the conference, it was hoped the official line would hold; Kirby had taken ill and Greg's mother had died.

The plan was to hire a Rent-a-Wreck and the officers would also have access to a departmental station wagon from Melbourne. This had private registration plates. These vehicles were at Mafeking Bay late in the week before the conference. It was assumed, if anyone even realised there were additional vehicles in the yard at the office, no one would associate them with the undercover mission and the duties about to unfold.

Lincoln was still regularly working the area around the lighthouse. While the officers did not positively know this, it was where Kirby and Greg initially looked on the first day of the conference. In a canary yellow boat, diving just below the public lookout for everyone to see, was Lincoln. Even without the aid of binoculars, the officers recognised Bernie Bowtell as crewman and dive attendant. The area was public and the activity very blatant. In Kirby's mind, this corroborated their intelligence about a departmental leak. He was sure Lincoln was confident there were no fisheries inspectors around to cause him grief.

Within a short time, observations were made of a catch bag being hauled aboard via the gantry. Kirby made his observations through a telescopic camera lense and Greg's were made through binoculars. Shortly after this Lincoln climbed aboard and the boat moved across the cove, past the lighthouse and stopped off the next point of land. This was a couple of kilometres from where the officers were so they left the carpark and travelled generally west through the national park. They then made their way towards the sea, the last part of the journey along fire-break tracks closed to the public. By arrangement with Mellissa, Kirby and Greg had keys. When they reached the cliff edge, they saw the boat again. It was now closer to shore than it had been before.

The cliffs in the area were pretty much devoid of decent vegetation to offer cover. There were eroded gravel areas and clay banks interspersed with windswept slopes, covered by tussocks. By lying on their bellies and only creeping forward when they felt confident the boat's occupants were not looking, the officers progressed to quite near the edge. To give himself more mobility Kirby left his camera case there behind a tussock. All the while Kirby took photos and Greg made notes.

There was a single box-thorn bush on the point and this appeared to offer an excellent observation post, if only they could get to it without being discovered. The bush was actually down a fairly steep slope, right on the edge of the vertical drop to the water. To get there required a slide down an exposed slope. Kirby went first and made it. Greg followed soon after. The bush was so small they had to huddle together in order to stay out of sight.

For nearly three hours they sat there. Every time the boat moved, it moved closer to them. Eventually Lincoln was directly under their feet and it would have been easy to shoot a marble onto the deck without duck fudging. When they were brave enough to take a peek they could count the abalone without binoculars. This was unbelievably good fortune, except for one thing.

Throughout the afternoon, Kirby took photos of abalone being taken aboard and all manner of other activity on the boat. At times the motor drive on the camera ran quite consistently. Had it had not been for the noise of the compressor on the boat, Kirby felt the whine of the camera's motor drive may have been heard by the pirates in the boat. He had already taken enough photos for a conviction and the officers were beginning to become bored. They were uncomfortable because of their inability to move or to do anything really, especially in relation to fundamental bodily functions.

Prior to the boat moving right in under the cliff Kirby announced he had nearly run out of film. There were several spare rolls, all in the camera case behind the tussock up the exposed slope! There was absolutely no possibility of getting to it.

The officers had no idea where Lincoln sold his catch. Earlier a licensed abalone boat had steamed past out at sea. While it did not appear the occupants even saw the yellow boat under the cliff, Kirby kept that last couple of shots on the last film in the camera. He reasoned if there was a transfer of abalone from one boat to another he would capture the evidence on film.

The decision to save the last couple of photos had been made before the last couple of times Lincoln moved his boat in under them. This meant there were no photos of abalone or Lincoln or Bernie when the boat was directly below them. It transpired there was no transfer of abalone and when Lincoln eventually left the area Kirby and Greg scrambled up the exposed slope, collected the camera case and ran back to the vehicle.

Lincoln continued to head away from Mafeking Bay to a remote and little-used boat ramp at the edge of the National Park. When Kirby and Greg arrived, they found the suspect vehicle with trailer attached, parked openly in the public car park.

They became anxious when their estimate of the time passed that it should have taken Lincoln to arrive. They waited and waited. Lincoln eventually steamed in as if he owned the place. Bernie Bowtell alighted and backed the trailer down the ramp behind Lincoln's station wagon.

It would have been easy to intercept the rig at the top of the ramp. At the time Lincoln was standing boldly at the helm of the boat as it emerged from the water on the trailer. Greg chose not to intercept then because, he reasoned, they had their evidence on film and did not have to rush. Besides, there were no police present and they did not know if the abalone were still on the boat. If Lincoln had brought the abalone back in the boat this may just present an opportunity to find out more about the marketing side of his business.

When the vehicle and boat left the ramp area, the officers followed it away from the National Park. They were in the Rent-a-Wreck and although cautious, did not expect to be detected. After a few kilometres Lincoln turned off the main road and into a farm. Kirby and Greg drove down a side road and waited. The suspect vehicle eventually re-appeared, minus the boat but heavily loaded. Kirby and Greg earnestly discussed whether or not this would offer an opportunity to gather some real evidence to prove the abalone were for sale. They decided they had to try.

They kept well back, hoping to maintain an undetected tail. This worked for a considerable distance, but in the next town they lost him.

For the next two mornings the officers kept surveillance on the farm house but Lincoln did not show. The location of the farm, as a hideout and launching pad for Lincoln's abalone poaching, was great information. As far as they knew they had not been detected, but perhaps Lincoln had been told of the two missing officers from the conference.

During the two days of waiting they convinced themselves their absence from the conference had indeed been reported. By Thursday evening the weather and sea conditions had deteriorated and they decided it was now time to act. They drew straws to see who would visit Lincoln and who would go to the farm.

Police assistance made up the raiding parties. Greg, with the assistance of one member, went to the farm and seized the boat. At the pre-arranged time Kirby knocked on the front door of Lincoln's house. Jackie Blewitt and another police officer were standing at his shoulder. Lincoln was very friendly but denied all the observations Kirby put to him.

'We have excellent photos. We were so close we counted your abalone,' Kirby explained. 'I am so confident about it all that your boat is being seized, and it's being seized at the farm where you left it. Officer Greg Bayliss and the police are there right now!'

This hit a raw nerve.

'Don't be so melodramatic,' Lincoln snorted.

By the time they left Kirby was positive Lincoln knew the note-taking and seizure receipt for the boat were not theatrical.

The next day, Greg and Kirby went to interview Bernie. He declined to comment on each allegation and observation put to him, and he did it with panache. Kirby thought this principled maintaining of his right to silence would have made Lincoln proud. Only when confronted with a sample of the photos did Bernie admit anything, and then it was only to admit the photos did depict him.

During preparation of the brief of evidence, Kirby and Greg relived the success of their venture a number of times. While the whole episode smelt strongly of the suspected leak, Kirby was never able to confirm it. Kirby knew Greg and Murray discussed the case at length via phone conversations, but if Greg had his suspicions as to the source of the leak, he did not relay them to Kirby.

When Kirby asked directly who it was, Greg turned his deaf ear and typically changed the subject.

'You know,' he said, 'Bernie is just about as good a crook as Lincoln now. Did you notice how he maintained his right to stay silent for just about everything? But the photos did the trick and he did answer the one meaningful question, didn't he? I suspect it won't make a scrap of difference in court but he admitted the one photo at least, was a photo of him.'

Chapter 16

The case was eventually prepared and the summons served. It was about eight months after the conference that the matter was listed for a contested hearing in court. Lincoln and Bernie were represented by Charles Ralph William-Peterson. The officers took this as a wonderful sign; Lincoln was one very worried pirate. In the past he had always defended himself.

Pleas of not guilty were entered by the barrister. After his evidence in chief Kirby was attacked during cross-examination.

'You don't really expect anyone to believe you were that close to my client's boat and remained undetected for such a long period of time, do you?'

This may have been two questions in one but there was no objection.

'Well, yes I do. It's the truth. When he was nearest to the cliff, we were virtually directly above him.'

'And you have produced over sixty photos to the court today, haven't you?'

'That is correct.'

'And there are no photos to depict your relative positions at the point you claim to have been above my client, are there?'

'No, there are not.'

'You're telling the court you didn't collect the best evidence available?'

'I told the court what I saw. That is evidence.'

'But you have no photo to prove it?'

'I have already admitted there was no photo taken when he was in that position relative to us.'

'You say you ran out of film. That's a very convenient statement, isn't it?'

The cross-examination went on and on. The basis of the defence became obvious; the officers did not, at any one time, see more than twenty abalone.

'Yes,' Kirby admitted, 'two divers could legally take twenty abalone. In all the time I watched though, the only person in the water was Mr Campbell. It would not have been legal for him to dive and take ten for himself and ten for his mate.'

When Kirby continued with this explanation of the law, he was no longer answering the question. All this did was attract an objection on the basis it was for the court to decide matters of law and not for a witness to tell the court what the law was. Kirby was chastised by the magistrate.

The lawyer continually asserted the officers had assumed they saw abalone because their specific task was to catch Mr Campbell taking abalone for sale. In the circumstances, he argued, it was natural for the officers to have a preconceived idea. Right from the very first moment they set eyes on the yellow boat, there was no doubt in their minds they would see abalone. The defendant was in fact catching Scutus Antipodes, a shell fish also known as elephant's foot or duckbill. In addition, he had taken wavy turbo and top shells. All these shell fish were for a number of part time Asian workers who performed manual labour in Bowtell's Boat Yard.

Mr Bowtell and Mr Campbell were pillars in society, not only employing refugees from a war-torn country, but also going to all this trouble to give them presents!

The story certainly contained some inventiveness but it failed to convince the court. The magistrate found the charges proven and announced severe penalties, including forfeiture of the boat. Lincoln immediately appealed on the grounds he was innocent and not the owner of the boat so, in the circumstances, the punishment was excessive.

As usual it took several months for the appeal to be listed and a date set in the county court. In the meantime, Lincoln and Bernie continued to go abalone fishing and they continued to use boats that were at the boat yard for repairs or service. An increased number of complaints and various sources of intelligence suggested this illegal enterprise had increased in frequency. In addition, the poaching was no longer restricted to the Mafeking Bay area. Kirby and Greg surmised this was because Charles Ralph William-Peterson was acting in the up-coming appeals and would be expecting his fees up front.

The department had its problems, too. The dilemma caused by the extraordinary level of poaching undertaken by these two required the department to step up a gear as well. These pirates had to be stopped, stopped soon and stopped once and for all.

Greg and Kirby worked up an operation plan that had, at its core, use of the police helicopter. The plan had a state-wide geographical area and because of their knowledge and experience, Kirby and Greg were the main departmental operatives for the campaign. Greg had a dislike for small aircraft and he insisted Kirby would be the one to fly. For once Kirby was delighted by Greg's decision.

A departmental memorandum of understanding with Victoria Police made all this possible. A date was chosen and written into the plan. The date was subject to weather and sea conditions as well as there being no urgent police need for Air 490 on the day. (They only had one helicopter at the time). Police command had an abso-lute and final say in the operation going ahead. The one saving grace in the whole plan was an option to engage the helicopter a second time in future. This opportunity could be exercised whether or not the first was successful, but again, police command had to sign off on one final last minute consent. Kirby and Greg both expected all to be aborted right up to the time the helicopter took off.

The first engagement followed a tip-off that Lincoln was working down around Wilsons Promontory. Kirby boarded the helicopter at Essendon Airport and flew directly to the prom where it searched around Shellback Island, past Tongue Point and then to Norman Island. It then flew back to the mainland south past Tidal River and Oberon Bay, out to the Glennie Group and south east to Wattle Island, then along the southern shore to South East Point. From here it returned along the mainland coast checking to make sure no boat had been missed. It landed to refuel not far south of the northern boundary of the national park.

Once refuelled, it headed south-east. This path took it over Mount La Trobe to Sealer's Cove. It then travelled south along the eastern side of the prom, out around Refuge Cove and Cape Wellington, across Waterloo Bay and down to South East Point again. Nothing.

Oh, well, it was a nice day for a flight so it headed the twenty five odd nautical miles from the Wilson's Promontory Lighthouse to the Hogan's group of islands, well into Tasmanian legal jurisdiction. They still found nothing. On the way back, as they crossed the shipping channel, they came upon a large container vessel steaming from west to east. It was directly in the helicopter's flight path, except for its altitude. The police pilot rectified that.

'Watch this,' Kirby heard over the hot-wired head set he was wearing.

The monstrous ship was un-laden, its bridge high on the square superstructure that reached for the sky at the stern. As the helicopter flew over the deck, Kirby looked up at the place where he knew the ship's captain would be looking down at the helicopter.

'You'll get into trouble' he spluttered.

'No, I won't.'

'What happens if he reports you to the Civil Aviation Authority? You'll lose your wings won't you?'

'He won't report me. If he does, so what? Who will believe a police helicopter flew across his deck below the bridge?'

Chapter 17

A couple of weeks later, Kirby got his second ride in the police helicopter. This time Lincoln was poaching down past the local lighthouse again. Bernie was his crewman and they were using a registered boat owned by a licensed abalone diver. The diver had taken the boat to Bernie for repairs and the only permission for its use had been an unspoken one in relation to testing the repairs when the work had been finished.

On this occasion Greg had teamed up with Jackie Blewitt and they were driving two different vehicles hired for the operation. Greg was in a fairly battered, light blue, one tonne Holden ute with a couple of hay bales on the back. Jackie was in a hired, near new Volvo sedan.

The two officers were in plain clothes and were pretending to be an item. They expected their disguise to be good, provided they were only observed at distances over one hundred metres. They were in a good observation position in the car park near the lighthouse. Both had cameras with telephoto lenses. From the top of the gully, both were taking photos as they observed the boat at anchor a couple of hundred metres away.

Lincoln did not personally dive that day but was obviously supervising three other people on the boat. They all dived, one on hookah and two on SCUBA. Bernie Bowtell was not there. As Greg watched, he made notes and took pictures. Jackie was taking photos and recording her observations by speaking into a tape recorder.

As pre-arranged, they used a portable police radio to contact the helicopter waiting on the ground at the northern end of the national park. It had been in a fenced off area around the works depot since arriving late the night before. This contact was the final all systems go signal.

'How good are your observations?' the pilot asked Jackie.

'They're good enough,' she said with assurance.

Air 490 was soon in the air with Kirby and a police forensic photographer as passengers. They headed directly for the lighthouse. As they approached Kirby saw the two vehicles before he saw the boat. The helicopter did a wide, high pass. After rounding a point well out of sight it dropped to below the cliff top and returned at speed. As it approached the boat the two cameras on shore were clicking and the tape recorder was rolling. Lincoln was on the boat and there were three divers in the water. The police tape recorder picked up Kirby's voice over the public address system of the helicopter. It was clearly audible despite the background wokka, wokka, wokka, of the helicopter's rotors.

'Lincoln Campbell, this is Kirby Wellington, Fisheries Inspector speaking from the police helicopter. Do not throw anything out of the boat. Recover the divers, haul the anchor and proceed at once to the boat ramp in Mafeking Bay.'

From the moment the helicopter had approached within camera range, the forensic photographer was taking photos from the elevated position. Afterwards it was remarkable to see how his photos showed exactly the same detail as those taken from shore. There was one of Lincoln leaning over the side deflating a parachute bag, one of the anchor rope being cut, and a series as the divers on SCUBA swam on the surface towards the boat.

Lincoln started the motor. When everyone was aboard he motored off at high speed. It was clear who was going to out-run whom this time! As the noise of the helicopter faded into the background on the tape, Greg and Jackie became aware Lincoln was not obeying the instructions boomed at him from the heavens. When the tape was later played, Greg was clearly heard ruing the fact the boat full of pirates was headed west, away from Mafeking Bay.

The tape was then switched off after a female voice could be heard saying, "They should drop a brick on the buggers."

The boat rounded the point and punched into a considerable south-westerly swell. On occasions it completely left the water. The helicopter was right there every moment, sounding the siren in long bursts, and occasionally with the pilot or Kirby giving unheeded instructions. One of the occupants later told Kirby being on the boat was like being in Apocalypse Now. Lincoln did not stop. The forensic photographer took some very spectacular photos out the helicopter window. One or two of these showed the **bottom** of the boat!

That boat ride would have been torturous. After some time, Lincoln turned and travelled back with the swells towards the lighthouse and Mafeking Bay. He then apparently realised speeding was pointless and he would never out-run the helicopter. He slowed to almost a stop. At times he did stop, sitting dead in the water until the helicopter approached to within a few metres. When this happened Lincoln would move off again. This cat and mouse game continued for well over an hour. As it did Kirby made radio contact to advise of the stalemate. The pilot did the same on the police radio. Kirby also relayed his belief the situation would not improve until someone on shore arranged to get a boat out there.

There were certain advantages in keeping the operation secret but one of the disadvantages was the complete lack of logistical support. Eventually the helicopter had to make arrangements to refuel. A twin engine aircraft, all the way from Essendon, relieved the helicopter, the pilot being another officer from the Police Air Wing.

Kirby and the helicopter crew landed and refuelled. They then waited the best part of an hour before receiving advice there was a boat on the way. It was a fisheries research boat from the Marine Science Laboratories at Queenscliff. It happened to be at Mafeking Bay, ready to begin some research project in the next day or so. Aboard were her normal skipper, a technical assistant and the other police member from Mafeking Bay. There was no fisheries inspector.

With this news, the helicopter left and proceeded back to the action or, more accurately, the lack of action. The chopper pilot made radio contact with the fixed wing aircraft that was still circling Lincoln's position. When the helicopter had visual contact with the boat, it relayed thanks to the fixed wing and again approached Lincoln at close range.

The fixed wing returned to Essendon and the same cat and mouse pattern developed. Kirby's feelings of frustration were now more difficult to suppress. This should not have been so because he could see the research boat approaching but knew this was not going to make Lincoln give in. When the boat arrived, the action became dramatic.

Lincoln saw the research boat and again gunned his motor to full speed. Kirby expected he would turn and run, but he continued towards Mafeking Bay, making the department boat turn through 180 degrees to follow. A certain degree of panic was now obvious on the part of the pirates in Lincoln's boat.

Kirby again spoke over the helicopter's public address system. He advised Lincoln to stop to allow the police member on the approaching boat to conduct an inspection. As expected, Lincoln ignored this demand. He also ignored the helicopter siren. The chase was now on again in earnest. The research boat, with its flying bridge not designed for ocean racing, was soon left behind. On the other hand, Lincoln had no way of losing or avoiding the helicopter. It followed the boat like a monster mosquito.

To the surprise of everyone on the helicopter as well as to those on the research vessel, Lincoln turned and entered the bay between Rocklyns Point and Point Alistree. Here the water was virtually dead calm and Lincoln travelled parallel to the Point Alistree shore. This course took him directly towards the outer edge of the large sand spit and shallow water on that side of the bay.

From the helicopter Kirby could see the shallow water and the direction of the chase. It was clear Lincoln was trying to lead the deeper draught research boat towards the shallow water. Kirby had begun to advise the skipper of the research vessel of the approaching danger when Lincoln ran aground. The decreased boat speed was abrupt. Lincoln tilted the motor to lift the leg clear of the sand, and as he did, a great spout of water shot skywards. With the throttle engaging full motor revolutions, the outboard was absolutely screaming.

The fugitive boat gradually began to move and the pursuing research boat was taking evasive action to avoid the shallow water and sand. In a short time, with his throttle fully open, it appeared Lincoln was about to leave the research boat behind again.

In the cockpit of the helicopter, and via both the police radio and Kirby's hand held, frantic communications asked if anyone could figure out what was going on. What were Lincoln's intentions? Where was he headed? How was he intending to avoid the interception? Surely he had run his race and was out of options. Mafeking Bay was not large enough to hide in.

Just then the helicopter pilot broke into everyone's thoughts and dropped a bombshell. There was a faulty instrument light on the dashboard, and no matter what, in five minutes he was leaving because he had to be on the ground by sunset. This was a legal requirement and there was no debate about it.

Kirby's heart sank and he felt defeated. In his despair, all he could think of was the amount of effort and money; and all for nothing. Lincoln certainly had a charmed life.

Just then, Lincoln stopped dead in the water. It looked like he had finally capitulated and the research boat advanced rapidly. Taking advantage of the situation, Kirby hammered out additional instructions over the helicopter public address system. He reminded Lincoln the police member on the boat had all the powers of a fisheries inspector and that he, Lincoln, was under arrest. Kirby knew this was not a legal arrest because it did not include touching the prisoner. He was so fed up with being disobeyed he did not care.

The research boat came alongside and the policeman stepped onto the pirate boat. At last things were working out but Lincoln had not surrendered. In truth Lincoln had to stop because he had run out of fuel! In reality Lincoln had been aware of his low fuel situation and his decision to return to the bay was based purely on this problem. He had not thought through anything other than his lack of fuel and now he was caught.

As Air 490 lifted away and headed north, the research boat took the pirates in tow. After the helicopter landed, Greg picked Kirby up and they were down at the boat ramp a good half an hour before the two boats arrived.

'You are all under arrest. You and you, over there, and you two over there! Move!' Kirby waved his arms giving directions as to who he wanted where. Each meekly complied. While there were two police members present, he had no idea what he would have done if they had disobeyed. Kirby told Lincoln to remain where he was until two additional police divisional vans arrived and all the offenders were transported to the watch house.

After the police processed the four offenders through the atten-dance register, Kirby and Greg went through the motions of formal interviews. Two each. All four gave their names, addresses and dates of birth. Nothing else, but nothing else mattered. There were pho-tos and good observations by departmental and police witnesses. Goodness some of the photos were even taken by a police forensic photographer!

While there was no actual abalone found on the boat there was flight. Kirby seemed to remember a high court case where prece-dence was set. The superior court held it was proper for a court to infer guilt in circumstances where the defendant's flight followed the appearance of authority. Kirby could not remember the name of the case but knew all about Lincoln's flight when the helicopter arrived on this occasion.

The case eventually came on for hearing in the magistrates' court. After two full days of contest, the court dismissed the charges of obstructing the helicopter pilot and Kirby. Charles Ralph William-Peterson submitted a no case to answer argument on the several obstruction charges. He contended there was no evidence before the court that the men in the boat heard the instructions given over the public address system of the helicopter.

In retrospect, the need for the prosecution to prove this element of the obstruction charges had been largely overlooked. To every-one involved that day it had been so obvious! Lincoln had heard what was said and the police helicopter was obviously there in rela-tion to offences being committed on the boat. Unfortunately the obvious was not evidence. The prosecutor unsuccessfully argued the court could take judicial notice that the public address system on the police helicopter was specifically designed so that people on the ground (or in a boat) could hear lawful instructions or advice from authority.

The police tape of the helicopter arriving and the audio recording of Kirby's initial directions was not tendered as evidence. As the prosecutor had said before court, the comment about bricks may be taken the wrong way.

'We don't brick people in court,' he had said.

The court agreed with Charles Ralph William-Peterson and dismissed all of the charges of obstruction against Kirby and the pilot. This came as very bitter tasting medicine. There were a large number of obstruction charges, beginning with the initial arrival on the scene, and then related to various other times and places as the day progressed.

On the actual abalone charges high monetary penalties resulted and the boat was forfeit. Lincoln was sentenced to be imprisoned for six months. Naturally, he appealed. The other three had no prior convictions and did not appeal their relatively low penalties.

This appeal, and the second one from the Swan Hill Conference incident, eventually came on for hearing in the Melbourne County Court. They were to be heard, one immediately after the other, with the decision on the first being announced concurrently with the decision on the second.

The photos on both occasions won the day and the charges were found proven. Despite all the trouble and all the prior convictions, the judge allowed the appeals in as much as the court varied the sentences. This was in no small way attributed to the eloquence and enormity of Charles Ralph William-Peterson's plea material.

During the period between the magistrates' court hearings and the county court appearances, Lincoln had suffered immeasurable personal misfortune. His parents were in a horrific accident that involved a tree falling across their bedroom when they were sleeping. They were both now in wheelchairs and Lincoln had taken over sole responsibility for their day to day welfare. This touched the judge and everyone else in the court room.

In allowing the appeals, the court announced all convictions would stand, but in relation to the case involving the yellow boat, a four year good behaviour bond would be imposed instead of a fine and goal time. The court also decided to return the boat, but this was conditional upon Lincoln "not parting with possession of the boat or motor during the period of the bond."

In relation to the second case, the judge appeared to be about to make a similar injudicious decision about that boat. The prosecutor had to remind him the boat had previously been forfeit three times. These orders were against the co-accused in the magistrates' court and had not been appealed. In this case the county court imposed a second bond of good behaviour for four years. It said nothing about the boat.

Outside court Kirby was livid. He certainly felt sympathy for the personal tragedy suffered by Lincoln's parents. That did not, in his eyes, lessen the extent of the offending. How could one measure the environmental damage wrought by this particular pirate? In addition to the direct impost on the fish resources, Kirby could not dismiss the untold cost and effort he and others had expended.

For once he almost felt sorry for the departmental bureaucrats. They had to pay for the use of the helicopter and fixed wing aircraft, for wages, for the hire of the cars and the use of the research boat. The more he thought about it the more expenses Kirby could think of. And what about the last laugh Greg had promised him? That was a joke Kirby did not find funny.

Chapter 18

For a considerable time after the county court decision, Lincoln kept out of trouble; but four years was a very long time.

About a year after the county court bonds were imposed, news filtered down from the Supreme Court. The first sitting day in May was set for the case lodged by the South Australian abalone diver, Adam Harvey. Kirby and Murray were to be represented by the Victorian Government Solicitor. He also represented the State in defending the action for damages.

Prior to the case even being listed, both parties had to exchange and file the documents they were to rely on in court. During the actual hearing Kirby was surprised how the only thing that happened was legal argument. This was put forward by both sides when the judge asked questions. When no evidence was given, and having not seen any statement other than his own, Kirby worried the court may miss some vital evidence or perhaps even miss some vital link to the fact this boat belonged to Her Majesty. This ownership question had been resolved in the county court well before Adam Harvey ever heard of it, let alone took possession of it.

It became obvious the court knew more about the case than Kirby. It proceeded to dismiss the case and awarded costs to the Victorian Government Solicitor. This seemed to be the first bit of good news for Kirby's last laugh, but he knew Lincoln had not yet retired from his illegal abalone fishing business.

After another elaborate planning exercise, an additional operation was initiated to catch Lincoln yet again. Another boat seizure occurred and this all cumulated with the next trip to the magistrates' court. Naturally, Lincoln contested the case.

In court on this occasion, Lincoln's defence was again conducted by Charles Ralph William-Peterson. This time the story placed the blame on three brothers, Aaron, Otto and Wesley Laudermilk.

After an abalone poaching incident near Cape Otway some years previously, these three had found their names in the little black books of the officers from Geelong. Subsequently they were on the department's offender data base. Aaron had disappeared from the radar since the initial case but Otto and Wesley had bobbed up from time to time with a conviction or two over the years.

In this latest matter, Lincoln's story in the magistrates' court contained a good deal of ingenious detail. He said he was aware the Laudermilk brothers, Otto and Wesley, had been abalone poaching and he knew where they had hidden their catch prior to it being retrieved. His curiosity had got the better of him and he was just having a look when the inspectors jumped out from behind the bushes and caught him handling the abalone.

The magistrate, not being convinced, proceeded to conviction. Lincoln followed his intrinsic modus operandi and appealed. Why shouldn't he? He had an irresistible version of events that would see him walk away from all but a couple of minor regulatory charges. To Kirby he appeared to handle the truth very carelessly.

The Laudermilk alibi had potential to be very serious indeed. The county court bonds would not be breeched until the completion of the appeal process in this most recent case. If a judge accepted Lincoln's evidence about the brothers, the department stood to lose the lot! Kirby thought again of Greg's promise about getting the last laugh. That was now years ago.

Since then, when Kirby was feeling low, he was of the opinion being a fisheries inspector was not meant to be funny or easy. This latest development in the Lincoln saga made Kirby more determined than ever; it would not be for the want of trying if Lincoln got away with this.

A few years prior to this case, the department had issued a summons against Aaron Laudermilk after Greg had caught him with a considerable amount of abalone. Otto and Wesley were not involved then but had always worked together since the original bust by the Geelong officers. They had adopted a unique ploy to avoid the full consequences of the law.

The younger brothers took turns accepting total responsibility for any abalone they were caught with. In turn, one would apparently make full and frank admissions and claim to have taken all the abalone. The other would deny any knowledge or involvement whatsoever. Without observations of what actually happened under water, the department's only option was to seize the diving equipment used by the brother who made the admissions. By taking it in turns to take the blame, and lose their gear, the brothers ended up with half the number of convictions and forfeitures they deserved.

Aaron's summons in relation to Greg's earlier case had been returned unserved. It carried an affidavit of attempted service stating, "After extensive enquires it appears the defendant has left the address and is now residing in Queensland."

In an effort to put an end to Lincoln's story regarding the Laudermilk brothers, Greg rang Brisbane and spoke to a contact he had in the Queensland Fisheries and Boating Patrol.

'Funny you should ask,' he said. 'I've got a case coming up soon in the Sandgate Court. I booked an Aaron Laudermilk for possession of a net on his boat. He is contesting it and on the night he had a couple of blokes with him. We half expect they will be at court to give evidence for him.'

Kirby and Greg discussed the description of these potential witnesses and Kirby was pretty sure they were talking about Otto and Wesley.

Greg contacted Murray Stephens in head office and discussed the need to interview Otto and Wesley. In order to counter Lincoln's defence in the county court, it was essential the department had written statements from at least one of the younger Laudermilk brothers. The need to prove the illegal abalone were not taken as claimed by Lincoln was obvious. It was expected a statement to show the brothers were in Queensland at the time, would do the trick.

Murray agreed, and Kirby and Greg flew to Brisbane to attend the court. All this happened during the 1989 pilot strike and it was quite difficult to get around Australia by plane. Somehow the two officers managed to be sitting in the Sandgate Court when Aaron walked in, alone.

After court began, they sat for half an hour or so, hoping against hope that Otto and Wesley would soon turn up. No one arrived. Kirby and Greg were both in civilian clothes and Kirby walked over and sat beside Aaron in the body of the court.

'Hello, Aaron,' Kirby whispered. 'You don't know me, I'm Kirby Wellington. I'm a colleague of Greg Bayliss who you may remember. You two met a few years ago over some abalone in Victoria.' Kirby indicated over to where Greg was sitting.

'What the hell do you want?' The tone of his voice and his facial expression clearly demonstrated surprise and annoyance.

'I need to talk to Otto and Wesley. I was hoping they would be here at court today.'

'Well, they aren't, and they won't be,' he hissed.

Kirby was very astute. He'd worked out by then Aaron did not want anything to do with him. Unfortunately for Aaron he was rather a captive audience and Kirby pressed on. He explained, in a whisper, his requirements in relation to Lincoln Campbell telling porkies about the brothers. He begged Aaron to call Otto and Wesley and get them to ring him. Kirby wrote the number of the motel where they were staying on a piece of paper and handed it to Aaron.

Having said all he could think of, he went back to sit beside Greg, miserable in the knowledge the trip had been a failure. Perhaps he was even more miserable when he considered Lincoln was probably going to get away with an unbelievable lie. The two Victorians sat waiting for the case to be called; there was nothing else to do.

Aaron defended himself. The Fisheries and Boating Patrol Officers gave evidence. On the night in question, they attended the scene of a boating mishap on the Brisbane River. Aaron's cabin cruiser had sunk, and during the salvage operation they had discovered an illegal prawn net on the boat.

Aaron did not contest this evidence and Kirby could see no possibility of him beating the possession charge. By not challenging the prosecution evidence, Aaron was admitting he did have the net. Kirby still had a bit to learn. Aaron's evidence went like this.

'I was steaming down the river and unfortunately got the propeller, keel and rudder of my boat tangled around a net which someone else had previously set. I knew it was illegal. Being an experienced diver from catching abalone in Victoria (that bit was true) I stripped off and dived under the boat and untangled the net. I could not just leave it in the river for fear another boat may catch in it too. I did my civil duty and put it on my boat.

'Unfortunately the force of the propeller twisting the net around the fittings on the bottom of the boat caused a plank to spring. I didn't realise this at the time, and as I continued downstream, my cruiser sank. I was actually really thankful the boating patrol people came along and helped me.'

The court dismissed the case. Aaron was happy but the Fisheries and Boating Patrol Officers were not. Greg and Kirby were not either.

As Kirby and Greg sat commiserating in the motel room that night they discussed what to tell the boss. They also wondered how they were going to get back to Victoria during the pilot's strike. In despair they began to discuss the upcoming grand final between Geelong and Hawthorn. Kirby barracked for Hawthorn and Greg Geelong. The phone rang. It was Otto and he was ringing from Townsville!

Kirby explained their predicament. They needed a written statement to the effect that he, Otto was not in Victoria on the day of Lincoln's detection. 'In fact we need you to be out of Victoria for a few days either side of the date.'

Kirby explained the accusation where Lincoln claimed Otto and Wesley had taken the abalone that had become the subject of Lincoln's charges.

Otto swore at the audacity but did not think he could help. The phone line went dead without warning. Otto had hung up. Then the phone rang again. This time it was Aaron.

'I've just rung to thank you for getting me off this afternoon.'

He genuinely believed Greg and Kirby had pulled some strings to get his case dismissed, but in return, he would not say how to get in touch with Otto.

Kirby figured if Aaron believed he could change a court result in the circumstances of the afternoon, then he could do the impossible and put a spoke in Lincoln's wheel.

He discussed his ideas with Greg. Greg was not impressed and told Kirby to forget the whole idea. Kirby was not put off that easily. Next morning, with Greg's blessing, Kirby rang Melbourne and spoke to Murray Stephens.

'We need to go to Townsville,' Kirby blurted out with no explanation. 'Can you organise the tickets?'

Murray obviously knew the purpose of the trip to Queensland and he calmly and quietly asked why. Kirby told him what had happened in court.

'Will it be worth it?' the boss asked. 'Do you reckon he will give you the statement?'

'I can't guarantee that but I think it's worth a go. If he doesn't it won't be for the want of trying. If I can't get a statement the possible consequences in the county court on Lincoln's appeal will be far worse than ugly.'

'I'll have to ring you back. What number can I get you on?'

Murray rang back within an hour.

'Your flight leaves Brisbane tomorrow morning at a quarter to ten. Your tickets will be waiting for you at the airport. You need to pick them up at least forty-five minutes before departure.'

'We'll be there, don't worry. Thanks.'

Kirby hung up and wondered if he should have told the boss they did not have an address or even a telephone number for Otto in Townsville. He hadn't been to Townsville since 1960 but was pretty sure the task would be much the same as finding the proverbial needle in a hay stack. The one thing encouraging him was the unusual family name. Surely there could not too many Laudermilk's in Australia, let alone in Townsville.

That day Kirby and Greg spent some time making contact with the Townsville office of the Queensland department. Next day when they stepped off the plane onto the Townsville tarmac it was hot. An examination of the Townsville telephone directory revealed only one entry in the name "Laudermilk." The officers checked out the address and found it was an old folk's home.

'Perhaps it's the mother or father of the brothers,' Kirby mused.

'One of them might have a job here,' Greg said. Kirby knew if that was true it would be a miracle. Otto or Wesley working in an old folk's home certainly did not appear likely. The receptionist was cheerful and helpful to a degree.

'No,' she said, 'Mr. Laudermilk is eighty-five years old. I don't think you are looking for him. He is not well and I'm afraid the whole place is locked down at the moment because of a gastro outbreak. This has affected both the residents and staff. Sorry, but I cannot let you in to speak to him.'

Kirby rang directory assistance and asked for the telephone number for Otto Laudermilk.

'He has recently moved up from Victoria but I don't know his address,' Kirby explained.

The operator gave the number of a new listings in the name of Laudermilk. The initial was not "O".

'You never know,' Kirby told Greg. 'The phone could be listed in his wife's name.'

Kirby rang the number but there was no answer. He tried every twenty minutes or so, and by evening, with still no answer, had become pretty despondent. They decided to give it a rest and try again in the morning.

Kirby rang the number quite early. It rang and rang. He was beginning to think the owner of the number had either left for work already or was perhaps still in bed. The latter proved to be the case. Finally Otto answered the phone.

'Good day Otto, its Kirby Wellington.'

'There were no beeps,' he observed. 'You're in town aren't you?'

'That's right. Can I come round to talk about a statement?'

'Hell, you must want him bad. Look, I've got to go to work but I'll be home for lunch. Drop round about twelve.' He gave Kirby the address.

When they arrived Otto, wasn't home. Mrs Laudermilk invited them inside but they declined and waited in the hire car. Otto was half an hour late but he eventually arrived. Kirby never thought he'd be so glad to see an abalone poacher.

Otto's greeting was rough but friendly. Over a cuppa and an enormous piece of rainbow cake, they talked. Mrs Laudermilk was very practical. The incident had occurred some time ago but she remembered what they had been doing. Their daughter's birthday was on the same date and this was a catalyst for remembering a whole series of activities.

Her recollection of the specific day was vivid; she remembered the names of friends who had helped celebrate their daughter's birthday. This helped refresh Otto's memory and the inspectors got their statement, including Otto's whereabouts on the days before and after the incident. It also included the fact Wesley had been at the party in Queensland. It was a hand written statement and Kirby faxed a copy to Melbourne. He and Greg then spent some time basking in their glory.

Because plane flights from Townsville to Melbourne were not frequent during the strike, they accepted an invitation from their Queensland colleagues and accompanied them on a boat patrol from the mouth of the Ross River out to Magnetic Island and back. When they arrived back at the patrol office there was a fax to Greg from Murray Stevens. He read it, then stood in stunned silence.

'What's the matter?' Kirby could obviously see something was desperately wrong.

'They say we have to get a second statement to corroborate Otto.'

Kirby then read the message. There was no doubt their earlier celebrations of success were very premature.

That night Kirby rang Otto and explained he needed a second statement.

'This has to be someone other than your wife. Would Wesley or one of the friends who were at your daughter's party vouch for the fact you were not in Victoria on those dates we talked about?'

Otto was pretty sure it was a waste of time talking to Wesley and he gave no guarantee about cooperation from anyone, but he did offer some help.

'Look, we are going to a spit at the Oonoonba Pub tomorrow night. Wesley and the mob from the party will be there. Why don't you come and I'll introduce you?'

Kirby couldn't believe there was such a place as Oonoonba. Otto spelt the name out for him about five times before Kirby thought he had it correct. He was desperate for a second statement and this was probably why he accepted the pub really did exist. On behalf of Greg, he reluctantly agreed to meet at the pub, half thinking they may have been set up for a bit of a laugh.

The next day was Saturday and the Victorian Football League grand final was on TV. The match began at 2:50 PM but the pre-match television coverage kept them entertained all afternoon. It was a brutal game with the lead changing several times. Hawthorn won by six points and the only thing detracting from Kirby's delight was Dermott Brereton receiving broken ribs.

That night Kirby and Greg took a taxi to Oonoonba. The pig on the spit looked fabulous but the pub's decor was not. The back bar had concrete block walls and a concrete floor. The decor included bolted-down concrete tables and concrete trestles. Grills covered the windows, the ceiling was unlined and the eaves uncovered. Kirby imagined on some Saturday nights the parties there would become blood-baths. He hoped tonight would not be one of them. He also imagined the morning after the night before. It would be easy to remove the blood, the mud and the beer from the bar with a good squirt from the fire hose.

As they waited for Otto's friend to arrive, they had time to speak to Wesley and some of Otto's other acquaintances. Obviously this was not the first time the brothers had been to the Oonoonba Pub! Kirby and Greg were very conscious of the dangers of joining the large shout that was under way and insisted they purchased their own drinks. As Otto predicted Wesley simply would not talk about giving them a statement. On the two occasions Kirby tried to bring the subject up, Wesley simply turned his back and began speaking to someone else. It was obvious he would not help in any way.

Eventually the potential witness arrived with his spouse and two small children. After the introductions, Kirby purchased drinks for the new arrivals. Together with Otto and his wife, they all sat around one of the concrete tables. After a very hesitant beginning, cold feet in the middle and some reluctance at the time of signature, Kirby finally had the second statement. It also put Otto and Wesley in Townsville on the date in question.

After making excuses for not staying for the spit, they gulped down the remainder of their drinks and left, returning to the motel via another taxi that happened to be dropping off some other patrons.

Kirby now had two reasons to celebrate, his footy team's success and the second witness statement to put paid to Lincoln's untruthfulness.

The next day they made it back to Melbourne despite the pilot's strike.

While they had been in Townsville discussing Lincoln's fibs about the origin of the abalone, Otto had sworn multiple times. He voiced his intention to ring Lincoln and give him a gob full. Kirby suspected he must have because a week or so later, Charles Ralph William-Peterson rang and advised Lincoln was going to abandon his appeal. The paperwork followed and this made the way clear for the department to have the learned county court judge deal with the breached bonds.

On the first day of these proceedings, Lincoln introduced Kirby to his mother. She was in a wheel chair and Kirby's immediate thought was not benevolent. *She's just here for another sympathy vote from the judge.*

'Oh,' she said. 'Your Kirby Wellington are you? Lincoln always speaks highly of you.'

That left Kirby gob smacked and he had a couple of small thoughts that Lincoln couldn't be all bad. The judge, however, did not have the same disposition towards him. While terms of imprisonment were not new to Lincoln, his appeals in relation to abalone offending had always kept him free on these charges. Kirby believed this was the first time he actually served time in goal for abalone poaching. The yellow boat was also forfeit.

The court listened in silence as Charles Ralph William-Peterson stood to detail his instructions regarding the yellow boat.

'A creditor, wanting his money, forcibly removed the boat from my client's possession. In my submission, the court should not apportion blame to my client for parting with possession of the boat, even though this was a bond condition. Your honour, I beseech you to see it is also not his fault that he can now not hand the vessel to the department. He instructs me he has no idea where it is.'

Lincoln did not have to give evidence regarding any of this. The good name and reputation of the legal profession were sufficient to convince the judge not to increase the punishment for that part of the breech. The barrister's client had suffered enough.

Chapter 19

The department soon dispatched a bulletin to all fisheries authorities in all Australian states. This communication included copies of photos and requested advice should the forfeited yellow boat come to notice anywhere in Australia. Again it was South Australia who came up with the information. A boat fitting the description was for sale in a boat yard in Port Lincoln.

Armed with a certified copy of the court order, and several copies of the previous judgement on the recovery of the boat from Adam Harvey, Kirby led another possie over the boarder to try to recover a second boat for Her Majesty. On this occasion, Murray Stephens and Greg Bayliss accompanied Kirby. They were both out for a junket and made no bones about the fact Kirby was in charge. They took two vehicles, a Toyota towing a suitable trailer and a sedan.

The night before they arrived at Port Lincoln, they stayed at Whyalla. Murray had the next shift in the Toyota and Greg and Kirby headed south well before daylight. They found the boat and crawled all over it. The only real life in town came from the seagulls and sparrows on their early morning jaunts.

It was the boat all right. The disguised exhaust system for the hookah still ran along under the port gunwale and the holes for the compressor mounting were still in the floor. They had brought with them a template of the mounting and the holes matched perfectly;

but the boat had a different motor. It was a new motor, a different brand and larger horsepower.

Kirby and Greg then had bacon, eggs and coffee at a roadhouse. Here they waited to meet the local fisheries inspectors as arranged. When they arrived, the South Australians had coffee too. They then took the Victorians and made appropriate introductions at the local police station.

A posse of two police and four fisheries inspectors invaded the boat yard. Right on cue Murray arrived with the trailer. This was just after the proprietor of the business had been given the good news about the yellow boat. He was only selling the boat on commission. He made a telephone call and not long after, the boat owner and his solicitor arrived.

The lawyer, with his chest puffed out, made some aggressive assertions about lessons in law if anyone tried to touch the boat. His attitude took a nose dive after Greg served the certified court order and handed him a copy of the previous boat forfeiture judgement. He read in silence, then called his client over into another part of the yard where they went into a huddle.

Soon after this the lawyer left the boat yard without too much more to say. Kirby and Greg went to work and removed the motor, using a block and tackle in the workshop of the yard. The craft had had some modifications and repairs carried out as well as the replacement motor. They made an inventory of these during discussions with the owner, who, by this time, had accepted his fate in very good grace.

They had the boat back in Melbourne one week after they left.

Chapter 20

While all this was happening, officers from Gippsland detected Lincoln up to his elbows in illegal abalone again. This occurred shortly before the court finalised his breaches of bonds and he was sent to prison. On this occasion, the officers had once more made good observations of the fishing operation and an unlikely relationship between the boat and a lady. To the casual observer, she was just sunbaking on the nearby beach.

At the completion of his fishing operation, Lincoln drove the boat to a different beach and left the abalone in the shallows, marked only by a piece of floating rope. Lincoln then casually walked along the beach, hand in hand with his female companion. Meanwhile the crew drove the boat to a third location. It was completely free of any real incriminating evidence when it arrived at the retrieval point. Watching and waiting nearby were additional officers, eager to seize it.

The officer in charge of the operation met Lincoln on the beach about the same time as the boat came ashore. He and Lincoln exchanged pleasantries, then the inspector gave Lincoln the good tidings of great joy. (Well, they were for Kirby when he found out.)

'Your boat is seized.'

Lincoln protested his innocence. After all, he was only having a relaxing day out at the beach with his lady friend.

'Lincoln, you should know by now we don't run you unless we've got the evidence.'

When this matter finally came before the court, Lincoln was still serving time in prison. Everyone expected him to get a goal order to attend court and to plead not guilty.

The department did not have the same legislative backing as police to prove prior convictions via an averment. Because of Lincoln's extraordinary number of priors, and their expected effect on punishment, Kirby was to attend just in case the prior convictions needed to be formally proven.

A lawyer contacted Murray Stephens and advised she acted for the defendant. She requested the matters be adjourned to the Magistrates' Court Melbourne.

'No way,' Murray answered. 'Most of our witnesses are from Gippsland.'

'You won't need your witnesses,' she said. 'He will plead guilty.'

'Will he admit his prior convictions?' Murray asked.

'Sure, he will.'

Murray agreed to the adjournment but made sure Kirby did attend court on the day. Right up until the time when he heard the lawyer say, 'My client instructs me to enter pleas of guilty your worship,' everyone from the department expected this to be some sort of stratagem on Lincoln's part.

The court proceeded to hear the summary and the details of a massive list of prior convictions before the solicitor presented the plea material.

She argued any custodial sentence should be served concurrently with the term he was now undertaking. The court disagreed and Lincoln received a six month term of imprisonment to be served consecutively. The court ordered forfeiture of the boat and Lincoln was fined very heavily.

As he travelled back to Mafeking Bay, Kirby thought back to Greg's prediction about the last laugh. That forecast had been a long time ago. Instead of feeling gleeful Kirby's countenance was more inclined to melancholy. What was the point? How much good had been achieved, especially when considered in the way of the bureaucrat? Where were the cost benefits and how did one measure them? All of the abalone taken by Lincoln and the other pirates ended up dead and not available to the environment or legitimate industry anyway. Did the political spin generated by prosecution statistics really mean anything to the environment or conservation principles?

'Kirby answered the telephone in the office the next day.

'Hello, Kirby, this is Lorren Bibby. You may remember me. I used to be Lincoln Campbell's girlfriend.'

Kirby recognised a very familiar voice from his past.

'I'm a bit surprised to hear from you,' Kirby said, the lump in his stomach developing remarkably quickly. 'Isn't there a little matter of time since a court case?'

'I know exactly what day it is. Don't worry. That's all over.'

The two chatted for a minute or two, speaking mostly about how, why and when she had left Lincoln. At one point she actually thanked Kirby for his part in getting her to see the truth; Lincoln was no good for her and they had been apart for over five years.

'Leaving him was the best thing I ever did and I have big plans for the future. You don't have to worry. You'll never see me in trouble with the law again. I'm working as a nurse's aide at an old folk's home. I'm studying to become a nurse and intend to give a bit back to society now.'

Lorren was totally calm and normal. When the call ended, Kirby checked the date. It was exactly five years and one day from the court date.

About the Author

In 1970, during the reign of Alfred Dunbavin-Butcher as Director of the Victorian Fisheries and Wildlife Department, Robert received a letter from the departmental head office at 601 Flinders Street Extension, Melbourne. It read, in part:

You have been appointed to the position of Fisheries and Wildlife Officer, Grade One, without additional salary.

The *without additional salary* bit didn't mean much at the time but the first departmental pay-packet ended any thoughts of returning to life on the farm where money from shooting and trapping rabbits paid for petrol, entertainment and a Coca-Cola on weekends. This changed financial situation occurred at the same time as Robert morphed to Bob; changing from mere mortal to Fisheries and Wildlife Officer.

When Robert received his offer of employment, Fisheries and Wildlife Officers were the shopfront of the department. At the time Bob had an ambition of becoming officer in charge at a country station and he still feels fortunate to have achieved this, in 1975, at Geelong.

After thirty-eight years working in the area of environmental offence management, Bob's effort to convert field work memories and fantasies into stories, has resulted in two books: *Are You a Bushranger Mister?* and *Pirates at Mafeking Bay.*

www.ingramcontent.com/pod-product-compliance
Lightning Source LLC
Chambersburg PA
CBHW070959180726
48291CB00004B/1363